# PAINS OF A MOTHER

BY

## HASSAN BARAKA

Edited by Winston Forde

Published by New Generation Publishing in 2020

Paperback ISBN: 978-1-80031-615-7
Hardback ISBN: 978-1-80031-614-0

**www.newgeneration-publishing.com**

New Generation Publishing

*In solemn reflection on the pandemic pain that has savaged most nations of the world
in 2020 arising from the relentless virus designated as COVID - 19*

# Acknowledgements

Pains of A Woman is based on a true story. However, the names of the characters are changed to hide their true identities. Many of my friends played a role during the writing of the book through talking and scholarly guidance.

I want to start by thanking my family especially my wife, Isatu Baraka, for their unconditional support. I also thank the following people for their invaluable assistance: Dr. Gibril Kamara, Professor Sheikh Umarr Kamarah, Dr. Malcolm Surrur and Dr. Victor Kabia.

Finally, many thanks to Dr. Philip Yamba Thulla for proofreading the manuscript and Sqn Ldr Winston Forde RAF Ret'd for editing the final draft of the manuscript and persuading me to adopt the actual locations in Sierra Leone.

# FOREWORD

I came to know Hassan Baraka through a mutual friend, Alhaji, who had read most of my stories, and had recommended me as a suitable proofreader with an honest, expert opinion. Without any hesitation, I agreed to read the manuscript, though mindful of the occasional bouts of headache I suffer during such close work.

I soon realised, for the first time, that the manuscript matched my kind of writing and interest. Hassan Baraka shares the same subjects and ethnological perceptions of life experiences about indigenous societies in Sierra Leone, as the ones recorded in most of my cultural stories.

The story centres primarily on a family divided against itself because of polygamy and sorcery, a subject, which Hassan shows to be at a dangerous extreme in the book. These practices have been glorified, criticised, corrected and dealt with otherwise by many writers, including my very self. The fact is that all of this is true, but there is far more to it than what a majority of writers have presented, even with the best of intentions. Less strongly is the fact that most of these practices have been shown to be in consonance with the religious and cultural observances of the Temne people.

Pains of a Mother is a well-written book that sheds its own light on this subject matter, with a rather new shade, in terms of shared traditions and expectations. I find it particularly impressive the way in which Hassan weaves the inextricable connection and the consequences that come afterward, into his story. This is an honest, true-to-life story that shows the unrequited pains African mothers go through to raise their children. Let Hassan take you along on this captivating epic journey into the society of the Temne people and by extension, the wider society of the people of Sierra Leone.

Dr. Philip Foday Yamba Thulla, PhD,
*co-author of 'The Chameleon Goes Home' and also 'Main man - the Memoire of a Thug.'*

# CHAPTER ONE

"Push! Push!" shouted Ya Yanoh, dressed in a mishmash of native Lappa and the white man's clothes. She was the famous *soweh,* as traditional attendants are called in Temneland. She lifted up a bundle of cowrie shells and hummed a tune.

"Confess your misdeeds!" she blared.

"Confess your misdeeds!" the soweh repeated, eyes fixed to an invisible deity.

"Is your husband the father of this child?"

"I have never slept with another man since I got married to my husband," Fatima muttered, sweat drops draining down her naked body. She gripped the sheet under her firmly, determined that she would give birth to this child, all her previous four babies had died at birth.

It was now five hours, the prolonged pain Fatima was feeling, together with the clanking sound of the soweh's shells, and her blaring sickened her more and more. The growling had called in more women, some topless, others clad in dark-coloured *lappas.* Among them was Yabom, Fatima's elder sister who started screaming immediately she saw her sister lying in a pool of blood.

"Keep quiet, miss lady!" Ya Yanoh commanded, irritated that her chanting had been interrupted.

"How can I? They have killed all her four children, but this time they will not succeed," Yabom sobbed.

"Do you want me to call her husband?" Ya Yanoh asked, slowly turning toward Yabom, "maybe your sister has something to tell him," she continued warningly.

"That ungrateful man thinks my sister is responsible for the deaths of their children and that is why he married other wives," Yabom paced the room, her lips quivering, her entire face contorted.

The argument had suppressed her anger. Ya Yanoh stopped chanting, walked into her bedroom and came back with a slimy concoction of herbs in a calabash. She used three fingers to scoop some of the concoction, which she shoved down Fatima's throat. Almost immediately, Fatima jerked convulsively, and a moment later she stopped bleeding, her water broke, and the baby's head popped out.

The other elderly women shouted together, "Push! Push harder!" Fatima squirmed, gritted her teeth, and pushed. The baby came out at the first cock crow.

"It's a boy," the soweh announced, shaking the baby gently and patting it on the back.

Despite her sore and bleeding state, Fatima observed the features on her precious new baby being briskly attended to and laid on her chest. The pain from her burning canal seemed less as she examined its pink, mottled skin, and chubby, bright eyes. *At best, he looks like his father*, she thought.

Fatima was just a seventeen-year-old maiden when she got married to Osman, an enviably good looking twenty-four-year-old man who had just completed Standard Five. He is now employed, doubling up as shop boy and clerk for Abess, a wealthy Lebanese merchant in the town of Lunsar. In addition to his looks, a well-paid job, including added benefits of provisions and rides in his master's car, made him a most eligible bachelor for almost all the young girls of Lunsar. He enjoyed this celebrity status and he boasted about it. It was a long time ago, but Fatima could vividly remember the day they met one very hot afternoon when her mother had sent her to the market to purchase some rice and onions. The moment she entered Abess' store, Osman had approached her.

"How can I help you, young lady?"

"I need rice and onions," Fatima said, counted the money and put it on the glass counter. Without taking the money, Osman brought out a small bag of rice, packed some onions on the counter and asked Fatima to take them home.

"I cannot pay for all these," she said.

"You don't have to pay," Osman replied.

"But I can't take them. My mother will be angry with me." Beads of sweat were rolling down her face.

"Who is your mother?"

"Ya Mabinty."

"Is she the one by the post office?"

"Yes."

"Okay just go. I will bring the rice and the onions this evening."

Fatima mumbled an answer, suppressed her fear and left. She proceeded to the market and purchased the rice and onions.

The memory of that meeting flashed in Fatima's mind as she turned to watch the soweh and the two midwives mixing another concoction for her. She'd yet to deliver the placenta, or afterbirth, so she turned over again to face the other end of the heavily decorated room. Animal horns dangled on the wall with bundles of broom straw set apart in one corner whilst piles of stalks and other implements were scattered about in full view. Fatima looked out of the window as a distraction, but she still could not force the image of Osman out of her mind.

Later that evening, Osman had arrived at Fatima's house with the food items honking the horn of his boss's car so loud as to attract the children at play outside. *That's Abess' car*, Fatima thought as she used a broom straw a short distance away in the compound. Osman ordered the shop boys with them to take the items in, but the loud honking of the car had equally drawn the attention of Fatima's mother who had rushed in to see what was going on. She refused both Osman's greeting and his gift, but her husband came out, greeted Osman warmly and instructed the boys to take the food items into his room.

From that day, the gifts became frequent and Osman succeeded in convincing the father to allow him to marry his daughter, despite the disapproval of his wife, Ya Mabinty.

They got married and Fatima grew to love Osman exceptionally. They became inseparable and Fatima became pregnant with their first child just after six months of marriage. Sadly, they lost the child soon after birth. They had the second and lost it, the third and fourth and lost all of them.

As they commanded her to push out the afterbirth, Fatima felt exhausted, disheveled and lacking in confidence. She had spent the last year alone with her pregnancy having to endure much painful taunting from neighbours and the co-wives, making her view the world as a place full of ingratitude, rivalry and turmoil. She had listened to songs relating to women who fake their pregnancies that caused her to hide in her room in the backyard. She had tried challenging such taunts by attacking her neighbours and co-wives verbally and sometimes physically, but each time her husband would rebuke her for doing so. Osman would beat Fatima often and on the day that she attended the midwife's clinic, the co-wives accused her of faking the pregnancy.

Yabom cradled the baby in her arms just beside her sister. "I am going to take you to the village to rest," she told her sister. "Your husband has refused to come and see the baby, but that is not important. I know he will come because there is no denying that he has fathered this child."

Without responding to her sister's comments, Fatima called for her snuff bottle. She took a pinch of the ground tobacco, tucked it in the lower left part of her mouth and passed the bottle to the soweh, who also took some and put it into her nostrils. She sneezed several times and her eyes became watery. "This snuff is very good," Ya Yenoh said between coughs.

"I'm sorry I scared you. This child is truly Osman's baby," she continued with delight.

The baby began to cry and Yabom handed it to her sister who immediately stuck her left teat into its gaping mouth. The baby sucked hungrily, and Fatima felt tears of joy streaming down her cheeks, for all her other babies had refused to suck her breast.

"There's no need to cry anymore," Yabom told her sister, "the important thing is that you are alive and the baby is doing fine."

# CHAPTER TWO

Osman still carried himself like a Casanova, with his wide shoulders flicked upward and his head tucked straight into his body. His dark hair was smeared with oil, neatly combed and parted slightly to the right like the tiny part on a baby's head. He walked into his room exhausted, not from his daily job but from the brisk frolicking he had enjoyed earlier with his third wife. He hurriedly kicked off his trousers, flipped it to a corner and threw his T-shirt on top of it. He reclined on his bed with a neat, but rough mattress.

The day before, his boss Abess had filled a carton of assorted provisions and given it to him to take to Fatima when he informed him, she had given birth to a baby boy. Abess also gave him the day off with pay. Instead, he had used this opportunity to lure his third wife, Ya Feth, into having a love session with him out of turn.

He was almost dozing off when he heard voices outside. They were loud and it sounded like women quarrelling. He sat up and listened keenly. They were those of Ya Baki, the second wife and his third wife, Ya Feth. Osman jumped from the bed, grabbed his trousers and hurriedly pulled them on. Without putting on the rest of his clothes he rushed outdoors to join the small crowd watching his wives in a mega quarrel. It seemed the moment that Ya Feth left, someone had informed Ya Baki that Ya Feth had been in Osman's room. The two wives were draped in similar traditional Lappas, the second wife was fat and visibly older than the third wife who was slim. She was clapping and ranting much more than her adversary.

"Is this your turn to be with our husband?" The second wife shouted, clapping her hands.

"Did I come to your husband?"

"For ordinary provision, Osman has ravished you. Shame! Shame!" Ya Baki moved forward as she spoke.

Osman rushed to defend his third wife, but the second wife stopped sharply, ran to the kitchen, grabbed a bowl and ran back without fear toward the third wife. Osman quickly stood between the two women and caught the content of the bowl on his face. He screamed as the hot water burned his face. He fought to open his eyes as he staggered around like a blind man. The onlookers burst into frantic laughter. Though they didn't like to see the two women fight, their laughter betrayed their approval of the second wife's latest action. However, few of them rushed forward to help Osman clean his face.

"Useless man," the second wife yelled, as she grabbed Ya Feth's Lappa and ripped it off.

She held on to part of her Lappa, pulled the remainder from Ya Baki and retied it around her half-naked waist as she slapped her right thigh to emphasise her point.

"Tell him to stop chasing me around. Blame him and not me, God has blessed me with a big waist and I will continue to use these hips to get what I want," she continued.

"You should be ashamed of yourself," Ya Baki replied and she followed the third wife, out of the compound, wagging her index finger in her face.

"You have bewitched our husband and that is why he is so attached to you," she raged and grabbed the throat of the third wife.

They struggled and crashed to the ground. The neighbours separated them and both wives got off from the floor, grabbing each other's Lappa and tugged hard trying to expose the other's naked body. The neighbours tried to separate them, but each time they did so the two women would pounce on each other. This went on until Pa Ali, one of the elders of the town, arrived and shouted.

"Stop fighting!"

The two women immediately let go of each other and quickly tied their Lappas back around their waists. Both were panting loudly.

"You must each pay a fine of fifty Leones right now," Pa Ali informed the two women. "You should be ashamed of yourselves, fighting in front of your children."

Both wives paid the fine and Pa Ali sent them back to their rooms. However, when Pa Ali left, Ya Feth started to taunt Ya Baki by singing the song that she knew she hated the most:

> She denied killing her mate's children
> She denied killing her mate's children
> But the witch doctor said she did
> But the witch doctor said she did
> In the end she confessed
> In the end she confessed
> She had to run away with disgrace
> She had to run away with disgrace
> O what a shame
> O what a shame.

"Our elders say, you cannot cross the river by simply walking along its banks," Ya Baki retorted as her mate continued to sing until she entered her room.

# CHAPTER THREE

There were no clouds over Lunsar on this quiet Saturday only a slight drizzling of rain that started the early hours of the morning. A gentle breeze blew the trees to one end. Yabaki sat on a bench in front of the town's chief crying and complaining between sobs.

"I did not sleep last night because of what my mate said about me,"

"What did she say?"

"She said that I killed Fatima's children," the chief winced.

"When I went to the market this morning, everybody was looking at me" she cried louder.

"Are you here to summon her?" the chief asked, thinking about her serious Accusation.

"I want you to come to our compound first and ask her if she had referred to me in the song."

"Okay I will do that. I will come there in the evening," the chief promised.

When Ya Baki had left, the chief summoned some older and respected members of the town and asked them to accompany him to Osman's compound in the evening. Since the rate at which Fatima's newborn babies were dying had been a concern among the elders and the people of the town, the chief also asked Yabom, Fatima's sister, to be part of his group and later they all arrived at Osman's compound.

Ya Baki had become impatient as she waited and the moment the entourage appeared, she rushed in to summon her husband who didn't go to work because of his injured face. Ya Feth was with him. After everybody had sat down, Ya Baki took some money from her Lappa and handed it to the chief who handed it to one of the elders to make the customary incantation before asking about the payment.

"I am complaining about my mate for accusing me in her song yesterday," Ya Baki said, tears streaming down her face. She explained how she had caught her husband cheating on her with her mate.

"When I tried to complain, this woman beat me up and accused me of killing Fatima's children," she said between sobs and blew her nose vigorously.

"God knows I do not have any hand in the deaths of her children," she continued.

"Let me explain why I said so," Ya Feth interrupted.

"No one gave you permission to speak," the chief interjected. "She is a senior wife to you. You should give her that respect and allow her to finish her complaint. You have to pay a fine of twenty Leones before we can continue".

Embarrassed by the rebuke, Ya Feth shuffled her feet and readjusted her head-tie to regain her composure.

"I am waiting for you to pay the fine," the chief commanded.

She unknotted the loose end of her Lappa, took out a creased Leone Note and pushed it into the hands of the chief. Ya Baki continued between sobs.

"God knows I have nothing to do with the deaths of Fatima's children."

"Why did you accuse your mate of killing Fatima's children?" the chief asked.

"It was a song I sang after she tried to kill me by squeezing my throat."

"And you mentioned her in your song?"

"Yes chief, but I was only taunting her," Ya Feth tried to apologise.

"So are you telling us that what you said that day was not about her?"

"Yes chief."

"Anyway, what you said that day about Ya Baki killing Fatima's children is still a very serious allegation," the chief stared at her sternly.

"I'm very sorry chief. I also want to apologise to Fatima and Yabom for what I said." The elders consulted and the chief announced his ruling.

"If a child is conceived during such an outlawed period, that child is regarded as an illegitimate child and there is the likelihood that he may end up doing certain things that would bring shame to the family. The ancestors, who are not happy about such a behaviour, may punish the illegitimate child in different ways in order to demonstrate their disapproval," the chief said.

"My children are all normal," Ya Feth muttered, feeling uneasy. She shifted her haunches on the stool repeatedly.

"The case in front of me is plain and simple. Osman is responsible for what happened and so is as guilty as his third wife, Ya Feth and both should be punished," the chief continued.

"Is it a crime to answer the call of my husband?" She asked in a trembling voice.

"You can always answer the call of your husband in an honourable way," the chief said, sat up straight and turned well enough to face her. "If your husband asked you to jump into a pit would you do that?"

"What you did is against our laws and the accusation you made is serious because it involves the loss of lives of four children of a co-wife," he continued.

"As I said earlier, what I said was not directed at Ya Baki. I did not refer to her in my song that day. I was just singing and all of what I said was not true. I was angry because of the way she attacked me," Ya Feth pleaded.

"What a shame," Ya Baki barked. The chief saw she was angry; contour lines were visible on her forehead.

"No one asked you to talk," the chief said. He too had started getting angry and Ya Baki thrust her Lappa between her legs and sat up properly.

Sensing the tension that had started to swell between these wives, the chief hurried to pass his verdict.

"Though you have withdrawn your wicked accusation, there is nothing we can do at the moment. The only way to prove the truthfulness of your words is to ask the help of a soothsayer who will be able to get to the bottom of it, just so that we appease Osman and Fatima who have suffered the greatest pain of the unexplained deaths of their babies."

"I think that is the right thing to do," said Yabom. Her chin was rested on the palm of her left hand.

"On the question of the fight between the two wives earlier, this is what I am going say," the chief continued, turning to Osman who had been silent since the case started.

"Before I say any more, let your third wife apologise now to her mate."

Ya Feth moved to the other end of the bench and turned away sulking. When the chief saw that she was belligerent, he gave a stern warning.

"If you refuse to apologise to your mate it will leave me with no option, but to double the fine I am going to levy on you."

The second wife, full of anguish, waited for the third wife to apologise. At least, she had been able to humble her. Not too long after, the third wife rose from her seat and grudgingly offered her apology to the second wife who, after some silence, remarked,

"God knows I have no hand in the deaths of Fatima's children. Wherever I go people look at me differently because of the remarks made by my mate. But I am happy she has taken back her words."

"Now, as a punishment for what Osman and his third wife had done," the chief said, interrupting Ya Baki, "Ya Feth is banned from entering her husband's room as his third wife for two months. In addition, she has to prepare the evening meal for two months."

On that final note the chief said his goodbye and left. The other elders got up from their seats, one after the other and followed their leader.

Osman felt devastated by the ruling as he had hoped for something more lenient. *Two months!* He turned away in horror as the full implication of the chief's punishment dawned on him.

However, Yabom felt rather pleased with the chief's proclamation. *Perhaps the truth is about to come out.*

# CHAPTER FOUR

Ya Baki got up early the next morning and hurried to the sacred shrine of Pa Saybom, the revered soothsayer of Lunsar. Contemplating throughout the night, she had concluded that the chief's pronouncement was sure to land her into a big mess. If she didn't move fast, her dirty dealing would be exposed. She knew how effective Pa Saybom's charms were. Not only was she worried about being exposed, the consequences in a town like Lunsar, where the mongering news could be as easy as mongering pepper, could be devastating.

So, this morning, she had come to do whatsoever Pa Saybom would ask of her. *It is better to pay for that than suffer the biting gossips of the people of Lunsar*, she thought. As she sat lazily on the bench placed by the wall of the kitchen hut, her mind drifted to her mate, Ya Feth. *"How could she do this to me?"*

When Osman introduced Ya Feth into the compound as his third wife, Ya Baki had readily welcomed her as a partner. She had trusted her with some life secrets, including membership of "Ansar", a group of revered witches in Lunsar. She had taught her everything and given her all the glories of the underworld, including making her to win the heart of their husband, Osman. Now she had refused to give back their husband. *I will get him by force*, she thought. The cranking of the door knob brought Ya Baki back in time. She got up as the door swung open and, as she had hoped, it was Pa Saybom who had stood in the doorway holding a Miller kettle.

"Good morning, great one," she greeted in Temne.

"Good morning," Pa Saybom murmured in reply. "What brings you to my shrine so early this morning?"

"I'm in trouble," Ya Baki replied, head bowed.

"What do you mean?"

"Ya Feth openly accused me of killing all the children of Fatima during the fight I had with her when I caught her cheating with our husband."

"It's just an accusation without any proof," the soothsayer replied calmly.

"No, it is more than that," Ya Baki argued, "the section chief who came to our compound for the mediation talks asked that a soothsayer be consulted," she continued whilst wringing her hands.

"What do you want me to do at this time?"

"Do not kill Fatima's child for now."

"It will require a big sacrifice to undo that," the soothsayer replied and started muttering some incantations.

"I do not mind the cost," the second wife replied with a sense of relief all over her face.

"Then you have to bring me two black cows, ten white hens, two dozen of white kola nuts, two dozen of needles and a role of white unstained cloth."

"Where will I get two black cows?" Ya Baki asked sounding desperate.

"If you bring the money, I'll find them," the soothsayer said.

"What will happen to the baby for now?"

"Something will happen to him later."

"When and what?"

"That I can't tell you now", the soothsayer replied. "It will depend on the outcome of the sacrifice."

Ya Baki remained deafeningly silent for some time, engrossed in the thought of what will happen to Fatima's child and at what time. However, she hesitated to ask too many questions that might annoy the soothsayer, a man of few words.

"After the sacrifice, I will give you a lotion that you will pour on the spot where you buried the items I gave you when you first visited my shrine," the soothsayer muttered in a bid to break the silence that had engulfed both of them.

"I definitely will," Ya Baki said submissively.

For a very long time, Ya Baki quietly nursed a deep grudge against the budding children of Ya Feth, who had become the favourite wife of their husband. Reacting to her public chastisement, Ya Baki decided to unleash her fury against the innocent children.

"There is one thing that I would like you to do for me."

"What is it again?" The soothsayer asked, looking quite astonished by another request.

"I want you to punish all of Ya Feth's children."

"Do you want me to kill them?"

"No, just render them incapable of doing anything meaningful in their lives."

"If you are willing to pay the price, consider it done."

"I am willing to pay any price."

"Then, it is done. You can go now."

Ya Baki left the shrine feeling confident that the soothsayer will not fail her. She had tremendous respect for his exceptional valour in rendering the almost impossible things that gave him the prestige he enjoyed amongst his peers. She still remembered a long time ago, how the soothsayer had solved the mysterious disappearance of a beautiful baby girl, killed by a jealous co- wife. The soothsayer had located the missing child in a shallow grave by the side of the river after searching diligently for a week, forcing the co- wife to confess to the grievous offence.

# CHAPTER FIVE

Fatima sat in a bamboo chair, with fingers clenched and a fixed gaze, as she watched her son play with the other boys. It was almost four years since she sought refuge with her baby in her mother's village. She had named the boy Salieu. Knowing the troubles she had gone through to save this one child, Fatima had always been very protective of him. She released her grip and forced herself to relax a bit more. The hide-and-seek the boys were playing had been too rough for Fatima's comfort, but she sat patiently, watching, not wanting to spoil her son's pastime. *Everything will be fine,* she told herself.

The sun struggled to disperse the bank of clouds gathering in the sky, as the atmosphere became gloomier. *It will rain soon,* Fatima thought. She did not want her son to get soaked as each time he got caught in the rain; he would shiver for the rest of the time. Fatima patiently shadowed him, but the rain never came, and the clouds slowly disappeared, leaving the sun to have the freedom of the sky.

She watched her son play blissfully and this helped to dispel the irrepressible fear that constantly lurked in her mind about the deaths of her other children before their first birthdays. Salieu had not shown any of the convulsive symptoms that had led to the deaths of her other children. Apart from the light fevers, Salieu was growing like a normal healthy child.

"Please watch your steps when running behind that shed," Fatima cautioned her son who enthusiastically ran past their hut, chasing the other kids.

"Why can't you allow the boy to play without bothering him?"

It was Yabom's voice and Fatima was quick to recognise it. She turned to where the voice had come from and saw her sister, carrying a basket full of things.

"Yabom!"

Fatima shouted, ran to Yabom and took the basket from her head. They held each other's arms and talked as they walked towards the family compound.

Fatima set the basket down, drew a bench close and let her sister sit on it. She went into her hut and brought out a cup of water and a bowl of rice.

"You can eat. After which you tell me what brought you here so soon," she said and smiled broadly.

"Salieu!" Fatima called, "your aunt is here." Salieu emerged from the back of the huts, crying.

"What's the matter?" Fatima asked.

"I stepped on a piece of broken bottle," Salieu replied. Fatima picked up her son, put him on her lap and carefully removed the piece of glass that was still stuck into the sole of his foot.

"That's why I wanted him to be careful when running. Here people throw away all sorts of things, in the backyard" Fatima sighed.

Salieu cried loudly when he saw the blood dripping from his foot. Gripped with fear, Fatima put her son on her back and took him to the kitchen hoping to find something that would help stop the bleeding. Yabom went to the bush behind the hut and got some herbs, which she held over the fire. Fatima took her head-tie, put the partially burnt leaves on it and wrapped it around the wound. Salieu screamed even louder and tugged on the Lappa of her mother. Soon, the herbs took effect, the bleeding stopped and Salieu fell asleep.

"He looks just like his father. That is why all the little girls are flocking around him," Yabom teased her sister, patting the boy's chin.

"I only hope he doesn't follow in his footsteps. He has not even paid us a visit since I came here with his son," Fatima replied tersely looking sad. "My husband is still ruled by that his witch third wife."

"That's what brought me here," Yabom said, softly. "The chief is calling on a sooth-sayer," she continued even before Fatima enquired.

"Soothsayer, for what?"

"Ya Feth accused Ya Baki of killing your babies," Yabom said and threw a pleasing glance at her sister, but Fatima was indifferent.

"I'm not surprised. I knew they were responsible, all of them," Fatima said, with a face looking pale with anger.

She sat and stared at the vacant sky. "But I'm not going back just yet," she continued, as she picked up the empty bowl and strolled into the hut.

# CHAPTER SIX

When Fatima came to Royanka, her mother's village, she was quick to open a small kiosk to sell liquor as a petty trader. Within a short time, the business blossomed because most of the young men who flocked to her kiosk did so with the sole purpose of making an impression on the lady from the town of Lunsar.

Most of them came well dressed in their khaki, or tar-gal pants with cutting edge lines. They would sprinkle the famous Bintu Sudan powder on the back of their necks and line the collars of their white shirts with white handkerchiefs for protection. Those who did not have the money to make impressive purchases, but wanted their presence felt would simply walk past the veranda where Fatima normally sat in front of her kiosk. They would either smile at her sheepishly, or wave discreetly and Fatima would reciprocate with a faint smile on her face, one that wasn't completely dismissive, but not in any way welcoming. Fatima did not encourage most of them and this became a talk of the village.

The discussions were protracted; all agreed that it was worth the trouble trying to woo Fatima whom they regarded as an extraordinary woman. All the men tried various other means to get Fatima's attention. In particular Amara, who often hunted came close, he used his catch as bait to do so. He would come with bush meat every day and leave it for Fatima. The children didn't like his practice of using meat to win *Yayo*'s heart, as they joined Salieu to call her mother, fondly.

They equally detested the teacher, a stranger they got to know as Mr Coker, who came to the kiosk every evening with his radio. Because he was from a big town, he was able to bond quickly with Fatima. He informed her of the latest news and the latest songs. He was always neatly dressed, with a round face and protruding eyes that sat prominently on his face, giving him an enviably pleasant look.

Every evening, the men of Royanka gathered at Fatima's kiosk but Mr Coker would always be the first to arrive and would nod his head in a rhythmic way and give a beguiling smile to the music from his radio. Yabom soon noticed that he had started to enchant Fatima and Salieu by his music and his unending stories.

"Talk is cheap," Yabom hissed in disgust each time the teacher left.

"You don't seem to like him?" Fatima questioned her sister.

"He talks too much, and he appears to know all the news in the world. Look at the way he proudly walks as if he owns this village."

"And is that wrong?"

"What bothers me most is that he does not buy anything from the kiosk apart from talk and he doesn't bring you any presents" Yabom observed dryly.

"But I do enjoy his stories, especially the one about Bra. Spider and his mother-in-law"

There was laughter from the crowd that started to gather at Fatima's kiosk one evening and it drew the attention of all. It was about the accusations of a man, as boastful as the teacher, about the predatory nature of the government and its stooges. Unable to challenge the teacher on national issues, the man changed the topic to village matters. His friends, some with partly covered bodies and others including Amara smartly dressed, supported the man, wanting to get back at Mr Coker. They spoke gleefully about the past heroes and villains of Royanka. Clearly, the teacher had met his match, and he listened uninterestedly.

Then, the discussion shifted to the recent burial of the oldest man in the village, Pa Wusu, whom many thought was a wicked wizard who had left many homes bereaved in the village. The old man was buried in the cemetery in the old town, located in a sparsely dense forest, a deathly silent place where one could hear the breeze whistle.

Rather unexpectedly, Mr Coker challenged the boastful man to meet him at the Cemetery at that ungodly hour.

"It is very fearful for somebody to go to a cemetery at night," Fatima cautioned.

"I will go there right now," the boastful man bragged.

"Then I will see how you are going to live up to your big talk," Mr Cocker said.

"I am not a coward as you are," the boastful man remarked, in a dismissive tone.

The place became tense and all the young men in the village wanted to see how one of their own would stand up to the stranger's challenge. Above, a full moon sat high in the night sky throwing so much bright light, that one could see one's shadow as one walked along. The teacher asked for a machete which Fatima gave to him. He went to the nearest bush and cut a stick, which he sharpened and gave to his contender.

"Since you are the bravest man in the village, you can go to the cemetery and put this stick on the grave of the old man," he dared him.

"How would we know that he indeed went to the graveyard?" Fatima asked, now interested in the game.

"We will know by the stake on the grave," they said, almost together.

Infuriated by the challenge, the man took the stick headed boldly towards the cemetery.

# CHAPTER SEVEN

Not wanting to appear a coward in the eyes of Fatima, the boastful man decided to run at full speed to accomplish the task. As he ran, the long rappel shirt he wore became bloated and when he reached the grave of the old man, he turned his back and plunged the pointed stake onto the mound. In his hurry, the stake caught part of his rappel. He struggled and the thought of him being held by the dead man echoed. He struggled more and wrestled against the invisible enemy. Then he dropped to his knees and slithered his lanky frame to the ground.

Back at the kiosk, everybody waited impatiently for the boastful man's return but when he failed to come back, they all concluded he had changed his mind and they left, one after the other, for their respective huts. Early in the morning, all the young men, including the teacher, visited the cemetery to find out if, indeed, the boastful man did what he said he'd do. When they arrived at the cemetery, they found the boastful man lying dead on top of the grave of the old man.

The death of the boastful man did not sit well with Amara. After checking his traps, he took the main road that passed through the center of the village to go to Fatima's kiosk. As he emerged from the bush, he saw two vehicles loaded with military men. They were armed with AK-47 guns. Both vehicles stopped and some of the men jumped down with the alacrity of a cat and approached him. One of the soldiers with a large scar on the left side of his face asked Amara in a hoarse voice,

"What is your name?"

"My name is Amara."

"How many miles is it from here to the next village?" the soldier continued his interrogation, in a severe manner.

"Have you seen a man by the name of Sorie?"

"No sir," Amara replied. He could feel his body shaking.

"Are you sure?"

"I'm sure sir," Amara said, eyes locked with the uniformed man. He looked like a big man and Amara regarded him as their senior as the other soldiers spoke with reverence to him, and they guarded him.

"The man we are looking for is the younger brother of one of the men that planned to overthrow the government, so anyone who helps to hide him will be in big trouble," the officer said.

One of the soldiers moved closer and spoke to the officer in a language that Amara could not understand. The boss then asked Amara to give him the bush meat he held in his hand. He kicked him hard on the buttocks and again asked how much Amara wanted for his catch.

"You can have them, for free" Amara replied. He was now terribly afraid, and his voice wobbled like a child caught stealing. Without thanking Amara, the soldiers climbed onto the truck and sped away, leaving behind a cloud of dust. Their next stop was Fatima's kiosk.

"We are looking for this man," the boss that interrogated Amara showed Fatima a picture. She was already very frightened as beads of sweat had started forming on her forehead. She saw the truck load of soldiers that held tightly on to the guns on their shoulders.

"I have never seen him before," Fatima replied, trying to calm herself.

"Are you sure?" the commander asked sullenly.

"I am quite sure."

Some of the soldiers clambered out of their trucks and helped themselves to cigarettes and drinks. Fatima knew they were not going to pay and for her it were better they didn't than they should pester her with such explosive questions and creepy looks. But this blatant act of transgression infuriated Mr Coker who had been wrestling with the fact that these were soldiers, or they were supposed to be, and as such should be comforting rather than transgressing. He decided to act.

"Are you going to pay for the merchandise you have taken?" he asked, holding his radio close to his right ear.

"Turn off that damned thing you are holding," the boss growled at the teacher.

"How can you ask us such a question?" another soldier, presumably the second-in-command, asked.

Mr Coker remained unruffled so the officers moved in a threatening group towards him, but he stood his ground in a stoic posture. The onlookers guessed that such bravery must either emanating from some hidden skill or depend on some influential political connection. Such thoughts were destroyed when one of the junior officers instantly hurled his truncheon, hitting the teacher violently on the head. He did so a couple of times before he spluttered a stern warning.

"Mind your own business and be watchful the way you carry yourself in this village."

The villagers were stunned by the brutal attack on Mr Coker, but they controlled their sneers. The teacher was speechless for a couple of minutes, rankled by the public humiliation over a question he thought was harmless. Now in pain and visibly irritated, he instinctively fired a prolonged outburst of denunciation as if possessed.

"What have I done to deserve this? You are officers of the law, and your duty is to protect us rather than intimidate us. This iron fist bestiality from men in uniform is incomprehensible. You have to stop this barbaric act of molesting defenseless people."

There was absolute silence at the kiosk as everybody was absorbed in what they considered to be a contest of willpower, between the boss of the military officers and the flamboyant and feisty teacher who was still standing his ground. This outburst stunned the officers, who were sure the obvious 'bookman' had rained insult on their boss even though they had no idea what some of the words meant.

"Can you make yourself a bit more understandable?" the boss asked, stabbing the truncheon in the air. But his prohibiting actions did not deter the teacher from speaking the more. He continued with his verbal attack.

"You know what you did is against the oath you took when you entered this profession. As men in uniform, your duty is not only to protect the government but also every citizen of this country. It is morally wrong to victimise people simply because they want their rights to be respected."

What the teacher said surprised the military boss. What annoyed him most was the applause by the villagers after the rain of words from the teacher.

"This man has book in his head," one of the admiring villagers said.

"Booker T. Washington," the officer said amidst laughter.

Inwardly, he felt battered by the unexpected impertinence of the teacher who looked undaunted by his adversary and the fiery looks in the eyes of the other soldiers. One could breathe the sullen expression on their faces. They never expected, in their wildest dreams, for somebody to publicly confront their commander, one whose authority was revered by the army.

In spite of the threatening stares of the soldiers, Mr Coker remained undaunted. All the young men in the village were amazed by such fearlessness. The soldiers surged forward toward the teacher but were restrained by a wave from their boss. The place became quiet again. One could feel the tension as the military boss looked at the teacher with a scowling face. He had a reputation for being short-tempered, but this time, he walked close to the teacher instead and placed the truncheon on the bridge of his nose, tapping it forcefully as he spoke. For some inexplicable reason, he maintained a façade of calmness which proved unfamiliar to his juniors. He stood silent for some time as if groping for words, repressing his anger, and spoke in an unexpectedly calm voice. This relieved the onlookers who were expecting a brutal onslaught from the officer.

"Nobody has ever challenged me in public the way you just did. However, I am not in the mood today to commit murder because it is my birthday," the boss said, gritting his teeth.

When the officers were asked by their boss to desist from attacking the teacher, there was a muted feeling of disappointment because they wanted to manhandle him and deflate his cocky poise. With orders from him, the driver hooted, and the throng of onlookers moved quickly off the road as the open van sped away, leaving behind a blanket of black smoke.

"You did a wonderful job by telling them the truth," Fatima said, and her son who had taken refuge behind his mother, rushed forward to shake the hand of the teacher. Though young, he knew the teacher had acted bravely and he was a fan.

"You are a very brave man," Salieu said.

"Thank you very much."

News about the teacher challenging the brutal military men spread quickly throughout the surrounding villages and made him an instant hero. Every evening when Mr Coker visited Fatima, he would spend some time with Salieu who now saw him as his role-model. He told him stories, taught him kindergarten rhymes and songs and helped him with his schoolwork. This closeness with her son endeared him to Fatima drawing them closer together as friends.

"The teacher is a nice man, and I will like him to be my teacher," Salieu told his mother.

"He doesn't live in this village,"

"Then take me to his school," Salieu requested.

"He does not teach kids. He will be your teacher when you grow older," the mother tried to convince her son, but he kept insisting that he wanted Mr Coker to be his mentor.

"When is he going back?" Salieu asked her mother.

"Within two weeks, but he has promised to come back every holiday to help you with your schoolwork," Fatima told her son.

"I hope so," the boy told his mother with a drawn face.

"Yes, and you will learn from him," Fatima further consoled her son

# CHAPTER EIGHT

Fatima's kiosk became busy again, but not for too long. A week later, the same army officers returned to the village and arrested the teacher. This day, they were more brutal, drinking packets of "Totapak", a locally brewed gin. The officers landed the teacher nasty kicks, yanked him to the ground against his will, stamped on him several times before tying him up.

This happened late in the evening. Most of the young men of the village were gathered at Fatima's kiosk listening to the evening news about the day's proceedings of the court, which many young men of the village thought was a kangaroo court set up by the government to try the "Coup" plotters. These young men had made an attempt to come to the teacher's aide, but they were rounded up and some received the wrath of the army officers. They knew that was in revenge for the public chastisement the soldiers received the last time from the teacher.

"Please leave him alone," Salieu pleaded but the military officers ignored his wild screams. They simply pushed him to the side and threatened to beat him up if he stood in their way again. Fatima grabbed her son and took him to the back of the house.

"He will be fine. He will be fine," Fatima reassured her grieving son.

"What crime have I committed?" asked Mr Coker still lying on the ground.

"I will answer that question when we get to Pademba Prison," said one of the officers who, seemed to be in charge this time.

"I am simply working on orders given to me by my boss," he continued, pacing about for no good reason.

"I need to know now. This barbaric act is against the law," the teacher protested.

This angered the military officers more as they were still mindful of the previous infamous encounter. They, therefore, beat the teacher more until he dropped on his knees, they then grabbed him off the ground and threw him into the waiting van. The crowd pleaded and screamed for mercy, but the officers just waved them out of the way, piled into the vehicle and sped away. Tears welled in Fatima's eyes as she watched her friend being taken away.

# CHAPTER NINE

Mr Coker felt piercing pains all over his body throughout the four-hour journey to Free-town. The road was terrible with endless portholes and the vehicle kept jolting its pas-sengers at every turn. The driver drove at maximum speed ignoring the terrible condi-tion of the road. The rope bit deep into the teacher's flesh and it gave him no chance to move. The army officers guarding him beguiled themselves with the most popular song in Freetown, *"THE WIFE OF MY BOSS"* while smoking Indian hemp. The teacher was sweating profusely, and the soldiers mocked and forced weed into his mouth.

"Try it. It will help you to overcome your pain," one of army officers joked.

The teacher coughed the weed out of his mouth, turned his face in a defiant mood and wheezed.

"Leave that fool," another officer mocked. "He is full of himself, but he will face reality when he arrives at Pademba Prison." The loud music continued and so did the journey. Mr Coker became frightened and for the first time the thought of losing his life came shattering in his head like a cascading ceramic ware. He had heard horrific stories of how prisoners, considered enemies of the state, were treated. Many were said to have been unaccounted for despite the persistent efforts of their loved ones to get information about their whereabouts. At this moment of somber reflection, Mr Coker started to think of a plan that would save him from a similar fate. *I must play by the rules if I want to stay alive and fight another day.* With this survival instinct pricking his mind, he kept quiet, but not about his pains.

"Why are you so silent now? You are paying for those nasty words you used against our boss," the military officer continued to taunt the teacher.

In a very contrite voice, the teacher asked the men to untie him. "The rope is eating my skin." There was tremor in his voice. His trepidation was palpable.

"Look at the way you are behaving now like a child," the leader of the group said.

"I was only trying to protect a defenseless woman," the teacher replied in a softer tone that he hoped would ease the ruthlessness in the soldiers.

"Shut up!" the officer roared. "Nobody asked you to speak. And if you dare repeat those words you uttered the last time, I will kill you and ask my men to throw you in the bush." He took his pistol from its holster, cocked it and pointed it at the teacher. The junior officers laughed when they saw the frightened look on their prisoner's face. He looked now like a rat that had been cornered by a cat.

"Please do not kill me," The teacher pleaded frantically.

"I did not know people who are learned can be so timid. I was expecting you to be brave when you are in trouble. So you were just showing off to impress the owner of the kiosk?" The head of the group said with laughter.

The teacher did not answer, and his silence angered the military officer even more. He kicked him until he became unconscious.

When they arrived at the Pademba Prison, they untied him, threw him into a cell and slammed the door.

News about the vicious arrest and treatment of the teacher by the military officers spread throughout the surrounding villages. The reason given for his arrest changed from one village to the next. In one village, people argued that the teacher was arrested because Fatima's husband, Osman, paid the military officers to assault him for flirting with his wife. Others alleged that the boss of the military officer who came to Fatima's kiosk the other day had planned to take Fatima with him but Mr Coker had tried to stop him. This last assertion looked more believable to people because it was a common practice for senior military officers to forcefully grab the beautiful wives of other men.

***

"I have to do something because my son has been unhappy since the teacher was arrested and it is having an effect on his health. He has lost a lot of weight," Fatima told Yabom.

"He will get over it. This is the way children behave when they miss someone they love," Yabom tried to downplay the seriousness of Fatima's concern.

"I thought so too but that is not the case, because it is almost a week and he has still not forgotten. He is still asking me where the teacher is, but I don't have any answer to his question and he thinks I am hiding something from him," Fatima said and bowed her head. She became convinced that she owed her son an answer, no matter how glib it might be.

# CHAPTER TEN

Unfortunately for Fatima, the baseless rumour about her dating the teacher who had been arrested by military officers reached her husband's ears and worsened the split between them. She wanted to go and find out what had become of the teacher, but something was holding her back. She had known for a very long time about her failing relationship with her husband, but she did not want to be the one responsible for its ultimate end. Even though she never had any intimate relationship with any other man, Fatima knew the rumour would give her husband the legal basis he required to get rid of her.

She thought long and hard and pondered on the wisdom of pursuing Mr Coker, which would definitely reinforce the false claim of a relationship with him. But this concerned her son and so she decided to take what she considered a justifiable risk. Her biggest challenge at the moment was where to start. She had not visited the capital city for almost ten years, and she had nowhere to stay.

"Do you know of anyone I can stay with in Freetown?" Fatima asked her sister whose countenance betrayed her disapproval of her sister's decision.

"No, I don't" Yabom replied grudgingly.

"I will take the risk, anyway," Fatima said.

"Where are you going to stay?" Yabom asked, "The city can be dangerous."

"I do not have any answer to that question. I used to have a friend, but I don't think I would find her where she used to stay" Fatima said.

"Then why are you taking the risk to go to Freetown that has so many problems?" Yabom pressed with the same air of apprehension.

Fatima was silent for some time. Despite her sister's effort to stop her from making the precarious trip, she had decided to go. *I must satisfy my son, and my conscience,* she thought.

"I am going to Freetown," she told her sister emphatically.

"In that case, I wish you all the best, my sister" Yabom said resignedly.

"Thank you," Fatima replied.

On the morning of the trip, Fatima took two Kola nuts, one red and one white, immersed them in a bowl of water and offered a prayer to her ancestral spirits for their guidance during her journey. She threw both the Kola nuts and the water toward the path leading to the road where she was going to board the vehicle. She wore a jaunty print dress with beautiful frills that looked nice on her. A pair of stylish earrings further complemented her simple if elegant appearance. Fatima's natural beauty revealed a very attractive woman, with neatly braided hair to boot. She walked briskly along the village path and soon she saw, one of the few vehicles that plied that route labeled "EVERYTHING NAR GOD." She waved a hand and the vehicle struggled to come to a halt.

"Where are you going?" asked the apprentice who was hanging precariously on the back bumper.

"Freetown."

"I am not sure if there is any space left but let me ask my boss."

The driver peered in his rear mirror and saw Fatima. *"The beautiful woman of the kiosk,"* he murmured.

"Find a place for her in the back," the driver told his apprentice.

"All the seats have been taken," the apprentice said.

"Come and sit with me in the front," the driver beckoned to Fatima smiling.

There were already two passengers in front, but the driver asked them to push to one side to make space for Fatima, much to their discomfort. When she clambered into the vehicle, the place was so tight that the driver had to ask her several times to adjust her sitting position. This allowed him to engage the gears dexterously. But Fatima did not mind the discomfort because vehicles were difficult to come by in the morning, and sometimes people spent the whole day waiting for one. She did not want to risk arriving late at the capital, especially when she was not sure of her accommodation.

During most of the journey, the driver looked at her with a glint in his eyes, but Fatima refused to take notice. However, the driver's frisky behaviour couldn't be easily ignored. To break the tense atmosphere, the driver asked, "Which part of Freetown are you heading to?"

"I am going to Portee," Fatima answered.

"Are you visiting a relative?"

"I am going to meet a friend of mine."

"I was born and raised in Portee. What is the name of the person you are going to visit? I might be able to help you locate your friend," the driver told Fatima.

"Her name is Fatu." Fatima used that name hoping that the driver would stop his queries. She used to know a friend by that name in Portee.

"I do not know her," the driver replied, scratching his head as if trying to prove the truthfulness of what Fatima had told her.

"I have not seen her for almost ten years, and I am not sure if she is still living in the same house," Fatima told the driver with an expression of uncertainty and uneasiness. The driver knew she had a problem and he resolved to exploit that.

They arrived in Freetown a little past midday and the number of people using the main streets had quadrupled. So, the vehicle competed both with other vehicles and with the pedestrians for access to the roads, sometimes making the driver to hoot his horns incessantly for passers-by to give way. It took Fatima two hours to travel from the out-skirt of the city to her destination, which to her was more onerous than the four hours she spent on the road to Freetown. She could hardly walk when she disembarked from the vehicle, feeling numb with cramped feet.

"Let my apprentice help you carry some of the load," the driver said.

"Thank you very much for your kindness," Fatima told the driver. She knew it would be a tactical mistake to allow the apprentice to accompany her. But she decided not to let the matter bother her. Instead, she concentrated on the daunting task ahead.

When they arrived at the house, she knocked on the door several times before a young boy opened the door, rubbing his eyes as if he had just woken up from a deep sleep.

"What do you want?" the boy asked.

"I am looking for Fatu," Fatima said calmly.

"Fatu!" the boy called out. A slim lady emerged from the house. She looked blankly at Fatima who equally looked blankly at the lady. They both were strangers to each other.

"I am looking for a lady by the name of Fatu, she used to stay here," Fatima said disappointedly.

"The people who used to live here left three years ago," the lady said with a smile, now sure the stranger was not hers.

"Do you know where they moved to?" Fatima asked, still feeling hopeful.

"I don't know," the lady replied. She was crestfallen. Her feet nearly buckled, but she managed to regain control of herself.

"*Where am I going to spend the night?*" she asked herself. While she was trying to sort out the cloud of uncertainty that hung over her, the apprentice stared expectantly. Fatima took some money from her purse and gave it to him.

Immediately, the lady asked, "Where are you coming from?"

"From Royanka," Fatima answered.

"You don't have a place to stay?" the lady asked, her eyes fixed on the bundles of food Fatima had brought.

"My sister went to work, but she will be home anytime now. You can talk to her to allow you to spend the night with us," the woman said. "You can come inside."

"Thank you," Fatima responded. As she sat in the tiny living room, she was unsure the lady they were waiting for would approve of her spending the night with them.

# CHAPTER ELEVEN

Mr Coker was taken to one of the cells designed to hold political prisoners. It was dark, but a dim light cast a faint yellowish shadow on the corrugated iron bars of his cell.

"Please help me," he yelled in a prolonged shrill tone, his voice echoing around the hallway.

"Shut up, you stupid fool and go back to sleep," one of the prison officers growled at him.

"Where am I?"

"You do not know where you are, you fool?" the prison office asked the teacher, "You will soon find out if you don't keep quiet."

"Please help me, I am dying," the teacher continued with his dogged plea.

"When you die, we will bury you in the prison compound," the prison officer said and smiled viciously.

"So I am in prison?"

"You are in your house," the prison officer said. "If you continue to disturb the peace, I will take you to another cell where you will not see any light for two weeks."

The teacher looked at the prison officer blankly, his body shivering with fear. Adjacent to his cell, another prisoner was jeering at the prison officer in an uproarious manner. His racket woke up the other prisoners who also joined in making giggling noises. Within a short time, a group of prison officers came and dragged the prisoner from his cell. The teacher could hear them beating him mercilessly. As the prisoner made doleful screams, so the officers beat him. The teacher was sure the officers were using iron bars to beat the prisoner. Not too long, the whimpering from the prisoner stopped, and there was deathly silence. *"They must have killed him,"* the teacher said to himself.

At Pademba Prison you could easily become a victim of misplaced rage. So, the teacher learnt without much instruction, that day.

"This is what we will do to you if you continue to disturb the peace," one of the prison officers told the teacher.

The beating reminded him of the one he received from the military officers. Now frightened, the teacher tottered to the far end of the cell where a dark brown bucket stood. It was a bucket toilet. He took a dirty blanket from the cold floor and lay down. He could not sleep because of the bedbugs. In the morning, three gallant prison officers came to his cell and took him to a hall. A man, possible a medical man, looked at him keenly, examined his wounds and ordered they take him back. A moment later, a Guard shoved an aluminium plate into his cell with a cup of water. It contained rice with a brownish soup and a ridiculous piece of fish. He could not eat the tasteless food.

"You will get used to the food," the prison officer told the teacher when he came back to collect the dirty dishes and saw that he had refused to eat his food.

"You have any money?" the prison officer asked. "You can use it to buy good food. That is what other prisoners do," he continued.

"I do not have any money," replied Mr Coker.

"Do you have anything to sell?" the prison officer asked.

"Only the things I had on me when I was dragged to this place," the teacher replied. He thought of making a friend out of this prisoner.

"I will go and find out if those things are worth anything, and then I will come back and inform you. I do not like the look on your face," the prison officer warned the teacher and left. This encounter startled the teacher, so he waited impatiently for a second, but the prison officer never came back. In the evening, two more prisoners were brought into his cell. They both had visible marks on their faces. They were not bothered about the state of the cell and in fact, lay down the moment they entered. When the same food was brought in the evening, they swallowed it and looked at the teacher who was struggling to swallow his own. They stretched their hands, and out of fear, the teacher pushed the plate to them. They thanked him and gulped down his food.

Early the next morning, the prison officer came with Mr Coker's belongings and told him the price a prison officer was willing to pay him.

"That is too small," he protested.

"You either take it or leave it," the prison officer commanded.

"What will I wear when I am released from prison?"

"Do not cross that bridge until you come to it," the sulky officer cited a familiar saying.

"You will be in serious trouble throughout your stay if you do not accept the offer," one of the inmates admonished Mr Coker who fixed his gaze on him and his tattered pants, his penis, swollen and headless.

"Do not waste my time," the prison officer barked. "You are lucky I got this deal for you and you are not appreciative of my effort." Frightened, the teacher reluctantly took the money and the prison officer left, cursing him for wasting his time.

"Now you can use the money to buy food or a bath," one of the inmates said, "I have not taken a bath for two months because I do not have any money. My sister who was helping me had an accident and could not support me anymore," he further complained.

"Do you have to buy everything?" the teacher asked looking bewildered. "The money that is offered to me is too small."

"If you want to be a privileged prisoner, you have to give them money. If not, life will be miserable. There are prisoners who have not taken a bath or gone outside for a whole year. That is too much to bear," the inmate explained.

The teacher waited impatiently until noon when the prison officer came to his cell. He felt lucky because it was the same prison officer to whom he gave his belongings to sell.

"Can you please get me some food?" he asked.

"If you give me the money," the prison officer said.

"How much money?"

"It depends, what you want to eat," the prison officer replied.

The teacher gave the prison officer some money, which he put in his back pocket without counting it and he left. A moment later, he came back with a bowl of rice and soup. The other prisoners watched in hunger. They were beckoning to the teacher, but he paid them no heed. The food was better than the meals that he got served the previous days. At this rate, the money he had on him could only sustain him for another three days, and the fear of starving to death haunted him. He could not sleep, and he envied his inmates who had resigned to their fates. He realised again that he was in big trouble. The conditions in this cell would break a man's will no matter how strong he resisted. He thought of Fatima and the sight of her son screaming when the military officers who were assaulting him shone before him. *"Maybe they have forgotten about me,"* he told himself. He fought to keep his mind away but the more he tried the more the incident refreshed.

# CHAPTER TWELVE

Fatima woke up when the owner of the apartment opened the door. She had had a short but deep sleep and she still craved one, for she was terribly tired. It was almost 8 pm and the neighbourhood was noisy.

"Who are you?" the owner of the apartment asked looking surprised to find a stranger in her apartment.

"My name is Fatima," she answered. The woman with the big waist emerged from her room and cut in with an explanation in Mende before Fatima could utter another word.

"She came looking for the people that stayed here before us, I told her they had relocated. But, since she came from Royanka village and it was getting late I asked her to come inside and wait in the living room until you come from work to make the decision whether you will allow her to spend the night here, or not," the woman with the big waist translated in Krio.

The owner looked at Fatima searchingly and spoke, "I had a meeting today and that is why I am late back. Have you given her any food?"

"She came when after I had finished cooking and the only food on the table is for you."

"You can give her mine," the owner of the apartment instructed her sister.

Fatima was enlivened by the hospitality, but she ate only a small portion of rice and gave the rest to the boy who earlier had answered her call.

"This boy eats like a pig," his mother scolded him as he swallowed the food.

"That is the way boys are. I have a six-year-old and he eats all the time," Fatima came to the defense of the boy. A feeling of nostalgia for her son gripped her and she inwardly started to like the boy.

"What brought you to the city?" the owner of the apartment asked.

"A friend of mine, a teacher, was arrested by the military and brought to Pademba Prison."

"What crime did he commit?"

"No one in Royanka could tell. He had an argument with a senior military officer who came to our village looking for coup leaders. A week later his men came and arrested my friend without any reason," Fatima explained.

"Many innocent people have been arrested and locked in prison because the country is under a state of emergency. Anybody opposed to the regime is locked up without trial. You have a difficult task at hand, but with money, everything is possible in this country," the owner of the apartment said.

"I do not know where to start and that has been my biggest problem." Fatima lamented.

"The first thing you have to do is to go to the prison and make sure he is there. Sometimes prisoners are killed to avoid overcrowding."

"I will do that first thing tomorrow morning," Fatima promised, but she was hesitant to ask her if she could stay in her apartment. "I brought some foodstuff for my friend but since she is not here, you can have them."

"Thanks for your kindness. How long are you going to stay?"

"It depends on how get on at the Prison."

"The only problem is I have only one room and I share it with my sister. I hope you do not mind sleeping on the couch in the living room."

"I don't mind at all," Fatima replied, breathing a sigh of relief. The owner of the apartment went into her room leaving Fatima and the woman with the big waste to get acquainted.

There was a knock on the door. Fatima's heart jumped. *"Who could it be? I hope it is not another unexpected visitor,"* she muttered. The woman with the big waste opened the door and saw the driver man standing there, holding a basket full of food and drinks. He wore a broad smile. "I am the driver who brought the stranger you have here to Freetown," the man said.

Fatima recognised the voice straight away and rushed to the door to enquire what had made the driver to come looking for her.

"Good evening Fatima," the driver said with a smile.

"Good evening," Fatima answered crossly. "What is the problem?" she asked.

"The apprentice told me that the woman you came to visit had left. I was worried and that is why I came to find out if everything is ok with you." the driver politely said.

Fatima gave the driver another scornful look. The woman with the big waste noticed Fatima's embarrassment, so she asked the man to come in. The driver entered the apartment and stood unobtrusively by the side of the door. He felt embarrassed too because Fatima did not give him the acknowledgement he had expected. He placed the basket on the table by the door.

"You can have a seat," the woman told the driver and entered her room.

"I am sorry for coming this late to bother you. The apprentice just told me you were having difficulty locating your friend and I wanted to make sure you were not stranded," the driver explained, still standing by the side of the door.

"Please shut the door. The mosquitoes are entering the apartment," Fatima told the driver, her eyes averted.

"There is a mosquito spray in the basket," the driver told Fatima in an affectedly decorous tone. He looked longingly at her.

"Thank you for being so thoughtful," Fatima said but carefully refrained from looking at the driver. She was still fuming inside because of his unexpected visit at such an awkward time when she was trying to settle down in her temporary abode that had been accorded to her. *Maybe the owner of the apartment will ask me to leave tomorrow?* She thought to herself.

"I will send the apprentice to check on you tomorrow after our trip from upcountry to make sure everything is fine with you. Good night," the driver said but Fatima's eyes were still glued to the floor.

"Good night," she replied. The driver left, gently closing the door behind him.

There was a tremendous buzz in the apartment and Fatima waved off the mosquitoes that intermittently landed on her ears. The heat in the living room was rising after the windows were closed. She took off her top print dress and stole a glance at the boy sleeping on the mat in the corner of the living room. She then reduced the flame of the paraffin lamp and removed the rest of her dress. The urge to examine the contents of the basket pressed, but she was still tormented by the sudden visit of the driver. She ignored her feelings and lay on the couch instead, but the buzzing couldn't make her fall asleep. Her mind started to wander. It drifted to the mosquito repellant inside the basket. She went to the basket, searched its contents, took out the spray and sprayed the entire living room. She choked and started to cough incessantly. The suffocation tempted her to open the window, but the horrible stories she had heard about thieves roaming the streets of Freetown looking for susceptible victims frightened her. To decompress herself, she went to the bucket, drank a cup of water and lay on the bare floor. The cement floor was cool, and she felt a bit better. She peered into the room of the owner whose door was ajar and saw her and her sister soundly sleeping on the floor, half naked. *So this is the trick*, she wondered. Fatima quickly removed the rest of her Lappa and used it as a mat. Not too long after she fell asleep too.

The noise of the shuffling feet of the woman with the big waist woke Fatima up. She quickly gathered her Lappa and sat on the couch. The boy was still sleeping, and the woman went and shook him violently, urging him to go and fetch some water.

"Your aunt has to take a bath before going to work," she yelled at him. "You will never wake up in the morning without me forcing you to do so," the woman continued to scold her son.

Still gripped by sleep, the boy stumbled out of the apartment and into the dark, loosely holding the handle of the bucket he had pulled from among the dirty pans.

"How far is the pump?" Fatima asked the woman.

"Down the hill," she replied.

"But it is still dark outside," Fatima said.

"If you don't get there early the queue would be too long," the woman explained.

Fatima put on her dress, took an empty bucket and went after the boy, worried something might happen to him along the way.

"You don't have to go after him. Nothing will happen to him," the woman shouted after Fatima who was already walking at a faster pace to catch up with the boy. When the boy heard the footsteps behind him, he stopped and turned frantically.

"It is me," Fatima assured the panic-stricken boy.

When they arrived at the pump, there were already people in the queue. The waiting was torturous, and the problem was compounded by children who were fighting for their turns; and the startling noise was irritating.

"Please shut up your dirty mouths," one old woman yelled from her window. "I will go and tell the owner of the pump to shut it down," she continued. Her threat brought sanity to the place and Fatima and the boy were able to fetch water.

"You can put your bag in my room," the owner of the apartment told Fatima when they came back from the pump. "How did you sleep last night?" she again asked.

"The heat was a problem, but I felt better when I lay on the floor."

"March is one of the hottest months in Freetown," the owner of the apartment said, "Do you know where the Pademba Prison is?" She continued.

"I meant to ask you this morning how to get there," Fatima said.

"It is in the Western part of the city and it is not difficult to find. But you have to start early if you want to get there on time. Catching a vehicle in the morning is not easy. Sometimes I have to walk to work."

"This is the reason I hardly go to town," the woman with the big waist joined the discussion. "Have you looked at the basket the driver brought for you yesterday?" she asked, moving toward the basket. "I think he is a nice guy."

"I did not expect him to come looking for me, because I've only been his passenger once and we hardly know each other" Fatima said.

"Drivers are like dogs and that is why I will never marry one," the owner of the apartment commented. "But they can be useful," she added.

When they checked the basket, they discovered an assortment of canned foods, sugar, milk and butter that surprised all of them.

"Please do not drive him away when he comes back," the woman with the big waist said, laughing to Fatima.

"But I do not want him to have the feeling that I am interested in him."

"At least you can pretend," the woman continued to plead with Fatima. There was a knock on the door and when the owner of the apartment peered through the window, it was the driver's apprentice holding a basket. She quickly opened the door.

"Good morning, madam," he greeted Fatima. "My boss told me to bring you this breakfast, and he will see you this evening when we come back from our trip upcountry," he added, handing over the basket and hurrying off without waiting for any response.

"We will see him in the evening," the woman with the big waist shouted after the apprentice. Without asking Fatima's consent, the owner ordered the boy to wash some plates and put them on the table. The food was dished out, and even Fatima was inwardly impressed by its quality.

"You do not have to cook today," the owner of the apartment told her sister. "This food is enough to serve us for the rest of the day," she continued, giggling.

"I hope aunty will stay with us for a long time," the boy said with an indulgent smile.

"All you think about is your stomach," his mother accosted him. "Hurry up and get ready for school," she yelled.

# CHAPTER THIRTEEN

At first ray of light, Fatima left for the Pademba Prison. Trips to the Western part of the city were disjointed and passengers had to board four different vehicles before they could reach their final destination. She stood for two hours without catching a vehicle. Each time one stopped, people would scramble to get into it, and they had mastered the art of doing so. Fatima lacked the necessary tactics to compete; especially with the school children who were quicker.

Exasperated by the overwhelming jostling, she hiked part of the way hoping to catch a vehicle further down the road. But, as she walked the stretch of the road, she realised that there were more people, including school children, trekking. After about three miles, she came to a lorry park where she boarded a vehicle. It was already packed with passengers.

The apprentice hit the side of the vehicle, as a signal for the driver to move. "P.Z junction, P.Z junction, P.Z junction," the apprentice announced his final destination. As they crawled along, the apprentice called out for more passengers. Fatima watched in awe as the driver manoeuvered the vehicle through the crowded streets.

*"There is no more space,"* Fatima told herself. But the apprentice continued to call for more passengers and those who did not mind the suffocating heat in the minibus clambered in. The experience was exasperating and so Fatima got off the vehicle to walk the rest of the journey to the prison. As she trudged and looked down the stretch of the road without seeing the prison walls, Fatima thought she had taken the wrong route, so she asked a pedestrian.

"How far is the Pademba Prison ?"

"Just continue walking straight on, you can't miss it when you see it," the man said without stopping.

*In the village, people took their time to explain things*, she thought as she continued her walk towards the prison yard.

Fifteen minutes later, the prison yard was in sight with its imposing high perimeter walls and bristling barbed wires. The Pademba Prison was a colonial legacy designed to hold only two hundred and fifty prisoners? At the time of the teacher's incarceration, there were over two thousand prisoners.

Apart from the severe overcrowding, the prison was also known for its poor conditions and the brutality perpetrated by its notorious prison warders. It stood conspicuously on one of the major thoroughfares of the city causing major traffic lock jams when high profiled prisoners were transported to and from the prison. When Fatima saw the huge forbidding walls with barbed wires, a feeling of overwhelming apprehension overcame her. She had never visited anybody in prison or seen a prison yard of any sort. She approached the massive solid metal gate of the prison with trepidation and banged on it.

"What do you want?" one of the prison officers asked as he opened a small window on the outer gate.

"I have come to see the teacher," Fatima said timidly.

"Visiting is only allowed on Mondays, Wednesdays and Fridays, from 11am till 2pm. Do you have a visiting permit?" he asked, piping through the small window, moustache jutting out like a brush.

"I do not have any," Fatima said.

"You have to go and get one and come back tomorrow," the prison officer hurriedly explained.

"Where can I get one?"

"Go to the Superintendent of prisons across the street."

Fatima wanted to ask another question, but the prison officer slammed the window of the outer gate shut. Stunned by the disdainful behaviour of the man, she retreated from the prison gates and without looking on either side of the road, rushed to cross. She halted when she heard the hooting of a car's horn. She had been missed. The driver hurled abuses at her and raced on. She headed towards the building of the Superintendent of prisons with diffidence, the uncouth behaviour of the building guard and the taxi driver rang in her head. At the gate of the superintendent's house, she was met by two dogs, who were barking, saliva dripping down their gaping mouths. The noise alerted the superintendent who came outside wearing a pair of short pants. He was short and bulky and with a turgid stomach.

"What can I do for you, young woman?" the Superintendent asked, scanning her from head to toe.

"I am looking for the superintendent," Fatima said with her handbag tucked under her armpit.

"You are looking at him," the superintendent answered firmly. "What Can I do for you?"

"I need a permit to visit my brother at the prison," Fatima said.

"Permits are issued on Tuesdays and Thursdays, from 8am to 12pm. You are late for today. You have to come back on Thursday," the superintendent explained and briskly turned his back on Fatima who instinctively looked at her watch as if to verify the time. The dogs swirled their long tails and resumed their loud barking. The superintendent turned and saw Fatima standing motionless like a statute. He was struck by her natural beauty.

"Where are you from?"

"From Royanka, but I was born in Lunsar."

"Did you say Lunsar?" the superintendent asked with astonishment written all over his face.

"Yes sir."

"My mother was born in Lunsar. Please come inside," the superintendent invited.

Fatima made an effort to climb the steps that led to the residence of the superintendent, but the dogs impeded her barking loudly. The superintendent ordered the dogs to go to the backyard, and they readily complied.

"Please have a seat," the superintendent requested, offering her a comfortable couch. "What would you like to drink?"

"Just water, sir."

The superintendent went to a freezer that stood almost the length of the dining room, took out cold water, some drinks and offered them to Fatima. She drank two cups and the cold water refreshed her.

"I have been to Lunsar several times, but I stopped visiting the town when my mother passed away. Who do you say you are visiting at the prison?"

"My brother," Fatima responded.

"Do you know why he was put in prison?"

Fatima explained in detail the brutal manner Mr Coker had been arrested by the military.

"I think he is in the remand section. There are many such people who are brought in because they are suspected of working against the government. They could be held indefinitely without trial because the country is in a state of emergency. I will examine his file tomorrow," the superintendent promised

Fatima could not believe her luck. He walked across the expanse of the living room and entered his office. Fatima scanned the engulfing living room that was impressively decorated with foreign items and furniture. Two pictures with golden frames hung on the wall. One of the pictures had the images of the superintendent, his wife and two innocent looking teenage girls, lavishly adorned in expensive jewellery. The other picture portrayed a dignified bearing of the superintendent in his uniform, slim and good looking; a complete contrast to the hippopotamus he had become.

Minutes later, the superintendent came back with the permit and handed it to her. "If you encounter any problems when you come tomorrow, just come and see me," he told Fatima whose eyes were still roaming the apartment in complete amazement of its luxurious decor.

On the signed permit was boldly handwritten, *"Please allow one hour of visitation time instead of the usual thirty minutes."* She took the permit and without reading it, carefully put it into her handbag, overwhelmed by the magnanimity and approachability of the superintendent.

"I do not know how to thank you," Fatima told the superintendent as she rose gingerly from the comfort of the couch that was draped in red shiny velvet. The cold water she had just gulped wallowed inside her empty stomach. The place was air-conditioned, and she felt the savouriness of the atmosphere.

"It is my pleasure to help you," the superintendent said affably.

Fatima replied with a smile as she closed the door behind her and walked buoyantly towards the street to catch a taxi. She felt extremely hungry and decided to stop by and get some food. It was almost 3 pm. She saw a restaurant with the bold writing, THE BEST CASSAVA LEAVES SOLD HERE. She entered it, ordered a plate and ate.

She arrived home late in the evening after trekking most of the journey.

"The apprentice just left here," the woman with the big waist told her without asking Fatima about her trip to the prison.

"What did he want?" she asked disinterestedly.

"He brought some foodstuff for you and bundles of firewood," the woman with the big waist said. "The driver is a kind man and I think he is interested in you,' she continued, pointing to the foodstuff in a big bowl to confirm her message.

Fatima smiled in gratitude, but her mind remained fully preoccupied with her next visit to the prison. However, the unending flow of kindness from the driver had captivated the occupants of the apartment and they now placed Fatima on a new pedestal of respectability, one that bordered on admiration. The owner of the apartment was now urging Fatima to loosen her face and treat the driver in a more dignified manner.

"Such men are difficult to come by in the city," the owner of the apartment told Fatima. "Most of the men I have come across want to be on the receiving end," she continued.

There was a knock on the door.

"Who is that?" the owner of the apartment asked.

"It is me, the driver. Is Fatima back?" He enquired.

"She just came back," the owner of the apartment answered, simultaneously opening the door. She shot a welcoming smile at the driver. "Please come in and sit down."

The driver sat in a chair by the door, a respectable distance from Fatima, but surreptitiously watching her contoured face.

"How was your trip?" he finally mustered the courage to ask her.

"I was unable to see my friend because I could not get a taxi on time to get to the prison," Fatima responded with downcast eyes.

"I have a friend who owns a taxi, and I will arrange with him to pick you up early tomorrow morning. How early do you want to leave?" the driver asked, his face beaming with confidence.

"Visiting hours are from 11am to 2pm," Fatima answered, this time looking at the driver, her face glowing with relief.

"Then he will pick you up at 9am," he assured her.

"Thanks very much for your help."

"It is my pleasure," the driver said. He rose and left in a lofty manner. He did not want to stretch things, but he felt confident that he was getting closer each time she accepted his services and he hoped this would ultimately translate to something intimate.

# CHAPTER FOURTEEN

The sudden twist of the fate of the teacher in prison puzzled him, and now he wondered in vain. In fact, the whole thing to him was an enigma and instead of making him comfortable, it made him nervous and disquieted. The afternoon, after Fatima left, the superintendent quickly passed orders to his subordinates to remove the teacher from his bug infested cell. Now he was being cleaned; given a haircut, washed, supplied with two sets of new prison outfits and taken to a new cell. Instead of sleeping on the cold floor with only a bare blanket, he had a mattress. Even the food he ate that day was of better quality.

"Have I got more money for my clothes?" he asked the same prison officer who had traded his clothes the other day.

"These are orders from above," the prison officer sneered and hissed in disgust. He said nothing more.

That night, the teacher could not sleep. Some of the inmates had told him that when the conditions of a prisoner suddenly changed without wangling or paying for it this usually heralded something sinister. The teacher, therefore, retired to a corner of the cell to ponder on such a prospect.

"This unexpected goodwill could mean that they want the prisoner to enjoy his last days before taking to the gallows. This is the only explanation I can think of," the other inmate had ominously told the teacher.

"Maybe they are going to kill me tomorrow," Mr Coker kept saying to himself. He could not come to terms with the scheme that suddenly gave him the status of a privileged prisoner, and that which had brought his sufferings to a head.

At approximately 11am, two gallant prison officers came to his cell and woke him up. Without saying a word, they marched him to the visiting room upstairs where Fatima sat edgily, waiting for him.

"You have sixty minutes," one of the prison officers said and moved a respectable distance from them. The teacher had observed that the prison officers usually stood within earshot, listening to the conversation taking place between a visitor and a prisoner, but the distance this officer had observed indicated he wanted to allow them some privacy.

"Good morning," Fatima greeted the bewildered teacher with a radiant smile on her face. "How are you doing?" He could read the astonishment on the face of Mr Coker.

"Things are much better today."

Mr Coker muttered, still trying to understand how such an unexpected visitation came about. He was, however, certainly happy to see Fatima again.

"Is it because of my visit?" Fatima asked, encouraged by the teacher's remark.

"Partly, yes," he confessed. "Since yesterday, my conditions changed. Did you give them any money?" The teacher asked with a smile.

"What do you mean?" Fatima asked.

"I had a bath for the first time Yesterday evening and got treated like a privileged prisoner. Some inmates were telling me to prepare myself for the gallows. I did not sleep the whole night. Now that I have seen you, I am at ease."

Fatima's mind quickly ran to the superintendent, but she could not be quite sure he had instigated the change even though her intuition kept confirming this. Since the teacher did not press on the issues, she quietly accepted the credit and changed the subject.

"My son extends his greetings to you," she said grinning.

"How is he doing?" The teacher asked excitedly.

"He is coping, just. Your arrest made him sad and he could not eat for a very long time. He asked me to come and see you to make sure you are doing well. From the cruel way they were beating you, he thought you would be dead by now."

"Please tell him I will go and see him as soon as I am released from here. All you have to do to keep me alive is to give them more money so that they will put me in the "GANG OF FOUR," Mr Coker beseeched Fatima.

"What is that?" Fatima asked, surprised by the mention of the word "GANG".

"That is a privileged group that is responsible for collecting the faeces of other prisoners from their cells," the teacher explained.

Fatima felt nauseated and could not understand how the teacher, a man she knew to be so brazen, would be asking for the opportunity to transport human faeces.

"Are you all right?" She asked.

"I know it sounds crazy to you, but this is the reality in prison. Those who belong to the "GANG OF FOUR" have the opportunity to go out of the prison walls and do menial jobs for the prison officers and other people interested in offering cheap labor. There are prisoners who have not seen day light or taken a bath for a whole year and it affects their state of mind. I do not want to belong to that group," the teacher explained and pleaded with Fatima.

"I will try my best," Fatima said, calming her apprehensive friend.

"Do you have a pen and a paper?" The teacher asked.

"No, I don't, why?"

"I want to write a note to your son." Fatima turns to the officer, took out some money from her bag and moved to him. She gave the officer the money and asked him for a pen and a paper. The officer rushed out and a moment later returned with the items and handed them to the teacher. The teacher spread out the paper on his lap, scribbled a note and gave it to the prison guard for his approval before giving it to Fatima.

"Time is up," the prison officer said with a surly face. He was stroking his moustache and from the manner in which he stroked his bushy moustache one could see that he was now snappy. Fatima gave the teacher a warm embrace and left the room with tears forming in her eyes.

They escorted Mr Coker back to his cell. The visit proved uplifting for him and he felt an inexpressible joy. The worry that had afflicted him throughout the night had vanished. He now felt assured of a ray of sunshine at the end of the proverbial tunnel.

Outside, Fatima briskly headed toward the house of the superintendent. The calmness of the place indicated an empty house and she felt disappointed. As she turned away, a vehicle suddenly pulled up in front of the house and Fatima saw the beaming face of the superintendent. He beckoned to her to come back. It became expediently clear to her that the charisma and beauty that men talk so openly to her about had lulled the superintendent into doing her biddings.

"Did you see your brother?" He asked as he struggled out of his car.

"Yes, I did, thanks" Fatima answered with a smile.

"How was the visit?"

"It went well," she said.

He invited Fatima inside and offered her another round of drinks. She kept quiet wondering how to introduce the topic about the help the teacher wanted without appearing too brazen. So, she beat around the bush, instead.

"I want to thank you with all my heart for what you have done for my brother," she said without looking at the superintendent.

"The pleasure is mine," the superintendent replied. "When are you going back?"

"I would like to pay him another visit before going back. Aside from that, he wants me to do something for him."

"What is that?" The superintendent asked peering erotically at Fatima who stayed silent, fidgeting with her purse. She raised her eyes and saw the pensive look on the superintendent's face.

"He wants me to help him join the group that is responsible for collecting the faeces of the other prisoners," she said.

"Instead of joining the GANG OF FOUR, I will allow him to work in one of the houses of the prison wardens," the superintendent promised Fatima. He went to his office, came back with another visiting permit and gave it to her.

Fatima thanked the superintendent profusely and left. She arrived home in a buoyant mood, glowing with the satisfaction that her trip to Freetown had not been in vain. She now believed, more than ever before, that her accomplishments would help to put at rest Salieu's fears.

While in Freetown, Fatima wanted to kill two birds with one stone. An acute shortage of rice existed all over the country and only those who were politically connected had the chance to purchase rice. The government used the "THE PAPER SYSTEM" to give unprecedented powers to the "Hajas," very important constituents in its political base. Through "THE PAPER SYSTEM", which the bearers had to present to government depots for rice to be sold to them, the "Hajas" made a lot of money by simply selling these paper permits to the highest bidders, who in turn sold them on to retailers at exorbitant prices. This syndicate put a stranglehold on the sale of rice. Artificial scarcities were created to hike prices to the detriment of the poor consumer. She recalled that at a time like this there would not be enough rice in her village and people would start to eat cassava and other tubers. But, her challenge at the moment was where to find the "Haja", sympathetic enough to give her a paper at a reasonable price. Late that evening, the driver came for his usual daily visits and during their discussions, the topic about the troubles people had to go through to be able to purchase rice abruptly came up. The owner of the apartment told the rest of the story. She narrated how a woman with her baby strapped to her back was crushed to death during a stampede. "No one could explain the miraculous escape of the baby who was still straddled to the back of its mother when the lifeless body of the woman was retrieved by the police," she concluded.

"To buy a bag of rice today is almost impossible if you do not have the right connections," the driver told Fatima, still shocked by the story of the woman and her baby.

"I wish to buy a few bags, but I think it's worth the trouble," she told the driver dejectedly.

"My boss knows one "Haja" whom I think will be able to help you," the driver told Fatima.

"I will very much appreciate it if you could get me a couple of bags," Fatima begged the driver.

The following day, the driver came with three bags of rice and gave them to Fatima. He refused the money from her and promised to take her back to her village whenever she was ready. After the driver left, the owner of the apartment told Fatima,

"He is a very good man. It is always nice to have a good friend in the city."

***

The villagers welcomed Fatima joyfully when she returned to Royanka ending the rumors that were already circulating. Some speculated that Fatima had gone to wed the teacher, and that she would not return. Others were saying that her husband got rid of the teacher and so would never allow her to return to the village and that her son was now being taken care of by her sister, Yabom. These rumours were the reason the shouting and jubilations reverberated when Fatima alighted from the vehicle that evening. Unfortunately, not everybody felt so pleased about her return. Amara's jealous wife felt anger and disappointment that Fatima had returned to the village. Salieu was happy, though and hugged his mother tightly. When she handed him the letter from Mr Coker, he peered at it as though he could read all that was written in it. Sadly, he could only treat it like a piece of toy as he moved around showing his friends the gift from his hero, the teacher.

That night, Fatima slept soundly, satisfied that she had resolved her concerns about the teacher that had pricked her conscience before she left to see him.

# CHAPTER FIFTEEN

Not long after her return from Freetown, Fatima's son became ill. This sudden illness caught her off guard and she knew evil forces were once more badgering her only son just as they did the others. But, she was determined this time to go the extra mile to protect the wellbeing of her son, even if it meant auctioning her last precious Lappa. And she did. When Salieu's health started to fail, he first had chicken pox that left indelible scars on his body, a black scar, the size of a pebble, stood on the topmost part of his chest just below his Adam's apple. Later, he developed an irritating skin disease that kept him itching and scratching all the time. Even when the herbalist in the village gave Fatima herbs to help cure her son's body, the irritation worsened.

"Why can't you take him to the hospital?" Yabom asked her sister.

"I think that is a good idea. I will take him to Mabesseneh hospital in Lunsar."

But that means taking him back to the same place where all your other children died."

"That is true, but do you know of another hospital that will be able to help my son?"

"There is one in Serabu. Those who visited it spoke highly of it, but that was a long time ago. I do not know the changes that have taken place in that hospital, but you can give it a try."

"I will go to Abess and ask him for help," Fatima said.

"Are you sure he will help you while Osman is still working for him?"

"He is a good man."

With this conviction, Fatima left for Lunsar. When she arrived at the shop, Osman sucked his teeth when he saw her. His face became sullen.

"What is the matter?"

"Our son is sick."

"You took the boy to your village for protection because there are witches in my house and now you are back telling me he is sick?"

"A child could be sick anywhere," Fatima said.

"That is why you should not have taken him to that village of yours."

"But I have lost four of my kids in your house, so that is why I decided to raise this one in Royanka. You have gone on to back your second wife."

"I have done what?" Osman asked aggressively.

"She might be right. I will give you the money to take him to the hospital," Abess interrupted.

With this help in hand, Fatima took Salieu to the recommended hospital in Serabu. For two months she watched him in deplorable hospital conditions. She cooked her own food and slept on the floor. Everything was expensive, so the day she did not give money to the nurses, her son would not get the attention he needed. Even though his body continued to deteriorate, Fatima never lost hope. But one morning, she faced the moment of truth when the doctor came very early in the morning to see her son.

"We have tried all sorts of treatment, but it appears your son is not responding to them. The lab in Freetown just sent me the result of his test which looks surprising," the doctor explained to Fatima.

"Is there anything serious?" Fatima asked.

"They could not find the cause of this skin disease."

"What do I have to do?" Fatima asked hopelessly.

"You have to take him abroad for more tests."

"Where will I get the money?"

"There is nothing I can do to help your son."

She wanted to ask further questions but the pain she felt inside forbade her to engage in what her intuition told her was a pointless discussion. Overtaken by the circumstances, she wept bitterly. She had only little money left. Her only option was to sell her Lappa and the set of gold trinkets, a priced possession that contained the family heir loom she had kept for a very long time. Without a second thought, she approached one of the nurses, sold the gold trinkets for a small sum of money and went to another hospital recommended to her by the nurse only to realize the outcome was the same. She left the hospital disappointed. After groping around for eight months looking for the right hospital to help her son, Fatima stumbled upon a woman with a conspicuous mole on her right cheek selling bananas at a lorry park. She had a child strapped to her back. After purchasing the bananas, the woman looked at Salieu with a genuine concern.

"What is the matter? Fatima asked the woman.

"What treatment are you giving him?"

"Why do you ask?"

"The skin disease of your son is similar to the one my son had."

Fatima became attentive. It occurred to her she had to listen to the woman.

"Will you be able to help my son?"

"I think I can. I'm sure that the old man who cured my son will be able to help you."

"How do I know you are telling me the truth?"

The woman lifted the tattered loose end of her son's shirt and showed Fatima. His whole body was covered in scars.

"If only you can make the trip, the old man will help you."

"I can go anywhere."

After a lengthy discussion, Fatima took some money and gave it to the woman.

"I do not need any money from you," the woman said.

This gave her hope that the woman could be real, unlike the ones she had earlier come across that took her money and gave her misleading information.

"*I have to find this old man no matter how long it takes me,*" she told herself.

Indeed, the journey to the famous native doctor proved very tiresome. After a day's long journey by vehicle on a treacherous road, Fatima and her son spent the night in a small village and the next day they continued their journey. They walked through a vast open land for about an hour. The dreadful heat from the scorching sun slowed them. Salieu rode on her mother's back for most parts of the journey, mostly using her Lappa to protect him from the rays of the hot sun. They finally entered a dense tropical forest with a charming collection of trees, which helped to cool their sweaty bodies down. Its thick dark trees stood several feet tall with overarching branches that formed a canopy layer above the narrow winding foot path that stretched for miles. The scenery was sublime. A mystifying eeriness grabbed them, and they immediately stopped talking. They walked silently for a long distance without spotting any sign of life. Suddenly, they beheld a tribe of monkeys frantically jumping from branch to branch as if excited about the presence of human beings. The monkeys scratched their heads and their armpits as they explored the branches, hopping, displaying their acrobatic skills like zoo animals playing in a gallery. Their persistent chattering became intensified and Fatima heard the distinct sound of the gong and she was sure they were approaching a village. The day quickly gave way to night because of the boundless overarching branches of the dense forest that blocked the fading light of twilight. It indeed gave the forest an undeniable mystic.

"The sound of that gong is unique, so we must hurry so that we do not cross paths with members of the secret society," the man assigned to escort them to the healer said.

"Do you know why they are beating the gong late this evening?" Fatima asked.

"I think it is the time for the gathering of the new initiates, or maybe an important person has died."

"What are we going to do?" Fatima asked.

"Let us hope that the next village is not too far because members of the secret society could be unforgiving if they are challenged," the man explained but then his mind drifted back to the time he was violently captured by members of the secret society and his father gave them the mandate to do even after his mother had protested.

The man hid himself in the rocks on the other side of the river bank with the presumption that the devil of the secret society would not locate him. Being a devout Muslim, his mother refused to tell the whereabouts of her son when contacted by the secret society members. They left without saying a word and within a short time, a heavy wind swirled where the boy was hiding. The boy had to come out of his hiding shaking like a baby. He was whisked off his feet and taken to the secret grove of the initiation. He spent seven years in the sacred grove. When he came back, his mother had passed away because of the rumour that her son had been devoured by the devil of the secret society. Despite the wealth of knowledge, he acquired during his long stay at the grove, the man hardly participated in the activities of the secret society because of the death of his mother. As the sound of the gong got clearer, the dense forest gradually thinned out and gave way to farmland, signalling their arrival at a village. There were people standing in their verandas as the man beating the empty shell of a tortoise paraded the length and breadth of the village announcing the sudden death of the chief in the grove of the secret society.

They spent the night in that village. There was singing and dancing the whole night.

"I thought the people are supposed to mourn the dead chief?" Fatima asked the man the following morning.

"The death of the chief was not natural," he said.

"What do you mean?"

"The chieftaincy of this village is linked to the secret society. When a person becomes a chief, he has to be initiated to find out if he is the rightful owner of the throne."

"I thought the chief was crowned after an election?"

"That is right but, sometimes those who are rich go around the rules."

After another long trek, Fatima broke the silence.

"I also heard that some members of the secret society have healing powers."

"That is true. Some members have healing powers but like all native healers, it does not mean they have the answer to all problems," the man replied.

Darkness had fallen when they reached the village, and their arrival was announced by the persistent barking of the dogs. The village was very small, and the house of the healer was noticeably big. It was the only house with corrugated iron roof with a large courtyard in which numerous goats and sheep were tethered. At the back of the house were three adjoining buildings that gave the compound a rectangular shape. Fatima and her entourage were met at the front gate by the head wife of the native healer who ushered them into the room of the old man.

He was seated on a mat. The room was dimly lit, and a string of paraphernalia of different mixture and tapestry gave the room a mysterious appearance. On the side of the bed was a big black earthenware pot placed on rectangular stones. It was emitting steam, but Fatima could not see any fire on it.

"You have strangers," the old woman told her husband who was meditatively counting a string of beads with his withered right hand.

"Let them sit down," the native healer responded without raising his head.

After a spell of uninterrupted silence, he finally raised his head and beckoned to Fatima to come close to him.

"What is bothering you?" The native healer asked with a guttural voice.

"My son has a skin disease," Fatima responded.

"Where is the boy?" The old man asked, hitting a shell-like instrument in front of him.

Fatima brought her son to the native healer who took off his clothes and examined the rest of his body. He stroked the boy's body repeatedly.

"I am sure you have visited several places to find a cure for him." the old man said with a grim smile on his face.

"That is right." Fatima said.

"An evil spell was cast on him," the native healer said.

"That is why I came to you for help."

"The only problem with this type of disease is that it will not be cured without a consequence," the old man said and grimaced.

"I will do anything for my son," Fatima said, tears rolling down her cheeks.

"When I cure your son, I will transfer the disease to you in the form of a mole, and it can appear in any part of your body."

"I will do anything for my son to get healed. How long will it take?"

"There is no time limit for this disease. It depends how fast your son will respond to the treatment."

"I will stay here as long as it takes," Fatima said, her mind drifted to the woman selling bananas.

"I will ask my first wife to give you a piece of land where you will grow some of the things you will need during your stay here with us," the healer said and concentrated on his beads again.

The man that brought Fatima and her son to the healer left the same day, just after the evening meal because he had a long journey ahead of him. Mother and son spent an uncomfortable night together in one of the rooms of the adjoining houses because the mattress was made of threshed rice stems. It was irritating to the body and Fatima had to sleep on the floor for part of the night. After the first cock crowed, which signalled the dawn of the day, she heard the chattering of women and their children. She peered through the door and saw a group of women getting ready to go to the stream to fetch water, others were pounding husked rice in wooden mortars with their children strapped to their backs. Others were holding hoes and cutlasses streaming out of the compound heading to their farms. Fatima heard a knock and when she opened the door, the old woman stood there carrying an aluminium bowl.

"You can use this container to go and fetch your drinking water. The river here is dry and we have to go to the next village to fetch water. Your son can stay behind today because my husband wants to start his treatment this morning," the old woman said, handing the bowl to Fatima.

"How far is the next village?"

"It's about three miles. You have to walk fast so that you can catch up with the other women."

Frightened by the prospect that she would get lost on the way if she did not walk with the other women, she stormed out of the room and followed the narrow, winding path that led to the next village. She came to a fork in the road and had to decide which way to go. Her mind went back to when she was ten years old, accompanying her mother to the village after having a confrontation with her husband. They left at the first cock crow and took an unfamiliar short cut. They came to a fork and did not know which way to proceed.

"Let us take the left side," her mother told her.

"Are you sure that is the right way," Fatima asked. Her mother stood scratching her head, not sure of which way to go.

"My mother always took the left turn on every doubtful fork and she was always right," Fatima's mother told her. Rightfully so, her mother took the right road because the right side of the fork led to the path where a famous chimpanzee was terrorising the people. It raped women and abducted young children. People believed that the chimpanzee was a wicked wizard in the village that had transformed himself because his land was wrongfully taken away from him. A famous hunter killed the chimpanzee after a prolonged reign of terror in the village and its environs.

*"I will take the left turn just as my mother and grandmother had done,"* Fatima told herself.

After a short trudging, she heard the other women laughing hilariously ahead of her. She knew she had made the right decision and exhaled in animated conviction that she had taken the right path.

Later in the day, the old man called Fatima into his room and her heart started beating fast, thinking that there was some bad news about her son.

"What side of the fork did you take this morning while going to fetch the water?" the native healer asked Fatima.

"I took the left side."

"That is a good sign. The right side of the fork takes you to the river but is twice the distance and it is a bad sign," the native healer explained while stroking his goatee white beard.

The compulsory work on the farm of the old man was back breaking. Every day, from cock crow to dusk, Fatima and other women toiled. When they returned, they prepared the evening meal. What made things difficult was that plots of land were apportioned to each woman and being a new endeavour to her, Fatima suffered greatly. Most times, she was the last to return home. Interestingly, nobody complained, despite the rigorous schedule, because it was engrained in the minds of the women that the survival of their children was linked to the work they were doing for the old man. There was one lady whose son was in a state of mental collapse when they arrived. He had to be restrained to a mango tree with a tight leash. But after months of treatment, the boy regained his bearing and the woman recounted this to motivate the others.

"I do not mind working from daybreak until dusk as long as my son is showing improvement," she constantly admonished the 'would-be-slackers' or grumblers. Because of the hard work in the farm, Fatima did not have enough time to nurse her own garden and she subsequently purchased things from the other women and soon she became cash strapped.

# CHAPTER SIXTEEN

Mr Coker served for an extended period at the Pademba Prison, so his services proved invaluable to the Superintendent. During his six years imprisonment, he helped to bring changes to the deplorable condition suffered by his fellow prisoners. He had the support of the superintendent who regarded him not just as a prisoner but more as a man of high integrity and profound intellect.

By a stroke of luck, his release came at a time when the superintendent's elder brother needed a principal for one of his schools. The superintendent's father started the school as a business interest and handed it over to his children after he had managed it for over thirty years. When the superintendent's elder brother took over control of the school, he expanded it and all the members of the family benefited greatly from the added income the business generated. So, the family members worked in concert to keep their successful institution going.

When the issue of the new principal was brought up during a family meeting, the superintendent did not hesitate to recommend the teacher as a most suitable replacement who would handle this popular school in the southern part of the country effectively.

"Are you sure he would be up to the task," the elder brother asked.

"I have been running the prison for thirty years, and Mr Coker is the only prisoner that has been innovative enough to persuade me to bring meaningful changes within the system. Even the prison wardens hold him in the highest esteem because of his brilliant ideas, which have helped to reduce the fighting of inmates in the cells."

"My only fear is that people would view him as a convict and might use that to undermine his authority," another member of the family said.

"The man was held without trial for six years. His only crime was that he challenged the authority of a military boss whose subordinates had victimised an innocent village woman. I have observed him closely all this time and he has not given me any reason to doubt his character. I think he will be an excellent choice for our deteriorating school," the superintendent proclaimed.

"Since you have observed him that long, I trust your judgment that he will be a safe choice. Does he drink?" The elder brother asked.

"I have not seen him drink, but that doesn't mean he does not," the superintendent responded.

"Okay, I will give him the job."

Three days later, the superintendent called the teacher and gave him the news about his new appointment.

"My brother has agreed to appoint you as the new head at one of our schools in Moyamba," the superintendent announced.

The unexpected good news shocked Mr Coker so deeply that he became speechless, as he gazed at the superintendent.

"Did you hear what I have just said?"

"I am simply lost for words," the teacher spluttered.

"You do not have to worry about anything."

"But I have never worked in the south, and I do not know how the people will accept me," the teacher mused.

"My brother has put in place the necessary conditions that will make things easy for you," the superintendent assured him.

But the fear expressed by the teacher was a genuine one. There was a deep-seated animosity between the people of the southern region and a government dominated by northerners. Before and immediately after Independence, the south held the seat of power. In the late 1960s and early 1970s, there was a shift in the political landscape and the political leaders of the south found themselves marginalised. The country had a one-party system dominated by the Northeast and Western regions of the country.

"I am sure you will encounter some initial resentment from them, but the moment they realise your worth, they will appreciate you and things will be alright. To be honest with you, the school is in a bad shape at the moment. I have no doubt, though, that you will be able to rescue it with your innovative ability," the superintendent continued whilst stroking the teacher on the left shoulder.

*** 

Before he went to his new assignment in Moyamba, Mr Coker decided to visit Fatima and her son, Salieu, to inform them about his new job. The superintendent asked the teacher to use his new vehicle for his trip to Fatima.

"I do not know how to drive," he told the superintendent.

"I will make one of my drivers take you where you are going."

"That is very nice of you," the teacher thanked the superintendent. In addition, the superintendent gave him money, which he used to buy gifts for Salieu, provisions, and other household utensils, for Fatima.

On their way to Royanka, the vehicle had to cross many police posts. At every stop, the driver would produce a card from his pocket and show it to the police. After a glance at it, the police would frantically wave the driver on their way.

"We are lucky today," the teacher told the driver.

"We are not lucky," the driver cut in, "They know the owner of the vehicle, that is why they are afraid to take any money from me," he continued with a smile.

They arrived at Royanka late in the evening, and Yabom came out to greet the teacher.

"Where are Fatima and Salieu?"

"Fatima took Salieu to another village because he is sick."

"Can you please tell me the village where she took him?'

"Yes I will." Yabom took her time to provide some directions.

Early the following day, he left in search of Fatima and Salieu and arrived in the village by mid-day. The sun was oppressively hot and half of the villagers had left for the day's work on their farms. The village comprised fifteen houses, built in a semicircle. Most had thatched roofs. The native healer's house was the first when entering and last when leaving the village. The teacher asked the driver to stop right in front of it. The native healer's eldest wife came out from the courtyard to greet the strangers.

"Good afternoon, what brought you to our village?" She enquired.

"I have come to see Fatima and her son, Salieu," the teacher replied.

"Fatima has gone to the farm, but Salieu is here."

"Can I see him?"

The native healer's eldest wife went inside and brought Salieu out to meet the visitor. When the boy saw the teacher, he sprang on him.

"How are you doing?"

"I am feeling much better. Let's go and see my mother."

Salieu grabbed the teacher's hand and pulled him toward the road that led to Fatima's farm, but as they were about to rush off, the old woman spoke.

"You can't do that. I will send somebody to go and get her."

The barefooted children, playing hide and seek game, came and surrounded the teacher.

"Go and continue playing," the eldest wife shouted and waved the boys off, but they ignored her, stood and waited for what the teacher was searching for inside the black shopping bag. He brought out some biscuits as gifts for the children. They sprinted away. The skin on the soles of their feet was hard and several cracks had formed on each of them. The bare-skinned boy the old woman had sent to get Fatima raced off and the teacher and the driver were ushered into the compound.

From a distance, Fatima's heart jumped when she was told of strangers who had come to visit her. She was not expecting anyone to come and visit her.

"I am not expecting anybody."

Fatima loosened her Lappa, retied it firmly above her breast, took her hoe and followed the boy. The distance seemed shorter to Fatima this time, for she was eager to see who had come to visit her. *Could it be my husband*, she thought as they got close. When they arrived, the superintendent's Land Rover was parked in front of the traditional healer's house. A moment later Mr Coker emerged from the back yard through the front door that was wide open. He was the last person she had expected to visit at the time. So, she looked in wonder at her friend, who looked immaculate if neatly dressed,

"Surprise, surprise," the teacher said. He gave Fatima a warm embrace.

"When were you released?" Fatima asked with excitement.

"One week ago."

"You are looking good."

"Thank you."

Salieu held the hand of the teacher like a magnet, swinging it back and forth.

"I bought you some toys and a bicycle."

"Did you say a bicycle?"

"Yes, a bicycle."

"Please let me see it, please let me see it," Salieu pleaded. The teacher brought out the bicycle from the vehicle.

"This is great," Salieu screamed.

"Do you know how to ride?"

"No, but I will start to learn today," he replied, his face beaming with smile.

"Thank you for the toys and the bicycle," Fatima said.

"Do people make a lot of money in prison?" Salieu asked the teacher.

"People do not make money in prison."

"Where did you get the money to buy a new car and all these things?" Salieu continued with his questions.

"You like to ask many questions," Fatima cautioned her son.

"Kids like to ask many questions," the teacher said." The car is not mine. It belongs to the Superintendent of prison, but he allowed me to use it. His brother has hired me as a principal to head his school in Moyamba," he further explained. "This is good news," said Fatima, with a broad smile.

"After your visit, things got better for me. With the help of the superintendent, I made quite a few changes to the prison."

"Now I can understand why the superintendent is so kind to you," Fatima said.

"But you are the source of that kindness."

"Can I ride my bicycle now?" Salieu requested, trotting the bicycle about.

"Yes you can," Fatima told her son, "but be careful."

The teacher spent two days with Fatimaa in the village and left the following day to prepare for his journey to his new workplace.

# CHAPTER SEVENTEEN

The journey to Moyamba was slow and jerky. The distance was not very far but, because of the police check points and their ceaseless harassment, the teacher arrived late in Moyamba.

"I cannot understand why the government is allowing all these police posts when they know that the police are not doing anything," the teacher grumbled.

"The police are poorly paid and the only way to subsidise their salaries is by allowing them to mount these many police posts. We are fed up with their constant harassment, but there's nothing we can do about it. The sad thing is that we have to take more passengers beyond what is allowed because we have to make up the difference," the driver complained. He was visibly bitter.

"What is disappointing is that they do not do their job. You can smuggle anything as long as you are willing to pay the price," the teacher commented.

The other two passengers, cramped in the cab of the passenger vehicle, shook their heads and moaned in approval. Moments later, the vehicle arrived at one of the major junctions that led to Moyamba. A police officer was shouting at the driver because he refused to stop at the designated spot.

"You refused to stop this morning and you want to do it again this afternoon. You have to get out of your vehicle and come to the booth. The boss wants to talk to you," the officer ordered the driver.

"I wanted to stop but the brakes failed me," the driver provided an excuse and looked at the police officer repentantly.

"Are you telling me that your brakes are not good? That is another offence," the police officer said, "you have to come and see the Inspector in the booth," he continued to order the driver.

The driver knew what it meant to go and see the boss. He was pondering his next move when the police officer left momentarily to go and stop another approaching vehicle.

"Why can't we just drive off? The police have no vehicle to chase us," the teacher whispered to the driver.

"My license and insurance have expired and if I leave without solving the problem, I will be taken to court," the driver explained.

After unsuccessfully pleading with the police officer, the driver left his vehicle and tottered toward the police booth. As he went, some passengers who had become very impatient, threatened to board another vehicle.

"All the passengers must get out and unload the luggage for proper examination," the Inspector told the driver and immediately entered the booth.

"Please sir...."

"I said all the passengers and the luggage must be removed," the Inspector interrupted.

When the driver entered the booth, other police officers were drinking palm wine. Two women were talking loudly and at the same time laughing boisterously as they drank their palm wine from big bamboo cups.

"Didn't you hear what the Inspector has just said?" One of the ladies asked in a belligerent tone.

"I heard him ma'," the driver politely replied, hoping that by doing so the woman would be sympathetic.

"Then why are you standing there like a fool," the woman retorted sharply to the bewilderment of the helpless driver.

"I want you to please help me talk to him for me," the driver pleaded with the woman in suppressed rage. He knew retaliation would put him in hotter water.

"Talk to him about what?" the woman asked in a tone that made a mockery of everything.

Disappointed by the bizarre behaviour of the woman, whose speech was slurred by the effect of the wine, the driver turned his gaze to the other woman who seemed interested in what was going on. She was about to say something when the Police Inspector interrupted in a high-pitched voice.

"Do not get them involved in your foolishness. You refused to stop this morning thinking that you are not going to return. This time you have to pay the price for your foolishness, and it will teach you a lesson, so you will not try that the next time,"

By the time they left the junction, half of the passengers had transferred to other vehicles. For the rest of the journey, the teacher's mind was preoccupied with the task ahead: restructuring a decadent school, lacking in academic performance and moral uprightness in an unfamiliar region. He knew the task would be monumental especially in a region not easily receptive to other people outside their strict ethnic group. But the superintendent's words still resonated in his mind: *they would accept you the moment they realise what stuff you are made of.*

He was determined to make a difference, so he entered the school compound with such zeal late that evening. He was shocked by the derelict condition of the school buildings. *"What have I got myself into?"* he asked himself as he stood gazing at the ruined structures. The main school building was a two-story house with several broken windows. The house tops were bare, with patches of torn louvers. Iron bars were attached to the windows and the scenery brought back memories of his early traumatising experience at the Pademba Prison. The other two small buildings on the left were made of bamboo sticks with corrugated iron roof. They looked like pig stalls rather than traditional classrooms. At the end of the school compound was a newly painted house with a house-boy's quarter, which he took to be the principal's residence.

"Welcome sir," a man of around thirty years came out greeting the teacher. He grabbed the bag and forced it off the teacher's shoulder.

"The Vice Principal and the Bursar were here the whole day waiting for your arrival. I will go and tell them that you are here at last," the man said animatedly.

"How far do they live from here?" The teacher asked, looking at his watch as if telling the man not to worry, it was already getting late.

"Not too far sir," the man replied. He was visibly happy. But the teacher knew the man was not being truthful in his statement and that he was simply trying to be nice to his new boss.

"Do not bother to go and call them because I want you to do something else for me," the teacher said.

"What do you want me to do for you sir?" The man asked.

"Who are you, by the way?" The teacher asked.

"I am the houseboy," the man said proudly.

"Right. Get me some water so that I can take a bath. I would like to go to bed very early tonight," said the teacher.

"The water is already in the bathroom. Would you like me to warm it?"

"Do not worry yourself. The weather is hot today and I prefer bathing with cold water. Thanks for the offer," the teacher said and smiled.

"Do you want me to do anything else for you sir?"

"I have some sardines in the plastic bag. The bread is in the other bag. Please make some dinner for me while I bathe."

"Yes sir," the houseboy said and left in a hurry.

Minutes later, there was a knock on the door.

"It must be that foolish bursar," the houseboy muttered. Instinctively, as he ran to the door and opened it. The bursar, his wife and her friend, Martha, who was dressed, as usual, in an enticing way had come to pay their respects.

"One of the students told me that he saw the new principal entering the compound," the bursar said.

"He arrived shortly when you and the Vice Principal left," the houseboy said. "But, he is taking a bath."

The houseboy took the basket the bursar's wife was carrying and grudgingly put it on the dining room table.

*"He has started his cunning tricks to gain favour from the new principal. I hope he will not eat this food because the man and his wife are notorious for charming people to get them to do whatever they wanted. How shameless this man is? He even came with another woman to trap the new principal as he did with the old, foolish, principal whose zipper was always down and could even sleep with a dog if it wore a skirt,"* the houseboy grumbled to himself.

Moments later, Mr Coker emerged from the bathroom, towel wrapped around his loins and was surprised by the unexpected visitors.

"Good evening sir," the bursar and his wife said in unison. "I am the bursar of the school and this is my wife and her friend," the bursar hastily continued before the principal could start asking questions.

"Good evening to all of you," Mr Coker said. "Please give me a few minutes to change. I was not expecting anybody this evening and please excuse me for coming out this way."

While in his room putting on clothes, Mr Coker's mind ran back to what he had heard before, about how people had used bats like women to entrap leaders in this part of the country. The woman who had accompanied the bursar looked alluringly beautiful representing the type that could enchant any man.

*"This is a trap, and I should not fall prey to it,"* he admonished himself and when he came out a moment later, the bursar made his offers.

"My wife brought you some food. She prepared it early this morning hoping that you would arrive by mid-day. The Vice Principal and I waited for you for a long time. I think you arrived moments later, after we left," the bursar said.

"That is absolutely right," the new Principal replied authoritatively, trying to assert himself in his initial encounter with the bursar.

"How is the road, sir?"

"As treacherous as ever."

"I do not know when this useless government will focus its attention on infrastructure. All the money they have stolen is enough to build all the roads in this country."

*Are you not part of the problem?* The houseboy thought. *You steal the school's money and go after little, helpless, girls and now you're blaming the ministers for doing the same thing. What naked hypocrisy! I hope and pray the new Principal would not tolerate your nonsense;* the houseboy continued to fume within himself.

"The road from Freetown to here is better compared to the one to Panguma. I traveled that road last week when I went to visit my mother. In some areas of the road, all the passengers had to alight and walk for a mile because the vehicle could not maintain its balance with all the passengers in it. The road is terrible. It took us five hours to do a journey of fifty-six miles," the bursar said.

"Are the parents of the head of state not from this area?" the teacher asked sarcastically.

"That is what is rumoured but other people are saying that his roots are in the north. We do not know what to believe any more and the president is using it to his advantage. The man is just too cunning," the bursar explained.

"The tea is ready sir," the houseboy informed the teacher.

He then brought the rice to the table.

"I like to drink tea in the evening," the teacher responded mildly.

"I will eat the rice you brought in the morning and please join me to thank your wife for me for being so thoughtful."

The wife's friend gave a beguiling smile in appreciation of the kind words of the new Principal and it helped to defuse the tension in the room between the bursar's wife and the houseboy regarding which food the teacher should eat that evening.

*Thank God, he has refused to eat their food,* the houseboy thought. *This will send a message to this foolish bursar that he cannot buy the new principal easily as he did the previous one,* he continued musing.

After drinking his tea, Mr Coker had a lengthy discussion with the bursar about the heavy task ahead of them and demanded that all hands should be on deck if the set goals were to be accomplished. The way the teacher approached the issue and the coherent manner with which he spoke left an impression on the bursar that the principal would be a difficult nut to crack.

"You will have my fullest cooperation, sir," the bursar assured the Principal after listening attentively to his briefing.

"Then I will see you tomorrow morning at 8am so that we will get the ball rolling. I have to go to bed early because I've had a very long day."

When the visitors left, the houseboy returned to his quarters quite pleased that Mr Coker had not fallen prey to the manipulations of the cunning bursar and his wife.

Moments later, there was another knock on the door. Mr Coker heard the knock faintly because he was already drifting to sleep. He was not sure whether it was real, or he was simply dreaming, but the persistent knocking jolted him out of his sleep. He got up and went to the door expecting to see the houseboy again.

"What is so important that he has to wake me up?" the teacher muttered. But when he opened the door, it was the friend of the bursar's wife, with a wide smile on her face that exposed the dimples on her cheeks.

"I am sorry to disturb you," Martha said politely. "I forgot my bag in the living room and I hope you don't mind me picking it up?"

"I do not mind at all."

The woman went inside and picked up the bag that was lying on the side of the sofa in the living room.

"I have the habit of forgetting my bag. Please forgive me for disturbing you," the woman said and smiled even more broadly.

"That's ok," the Principal replied curtly.

When the houseboy heard the loud knocks on the door of the principal, he came back to investigate the problem. By the time he got to the door, the Principal had already opened it for the woman. Aghast by the development, the houseboy quietly retreated and squatted by the side of the house, eavesdropping on their conversation.

"W*hat a harlot,*" the houseboy fumed ungraciously. "*She has come back to sell herself to the teacher and the poor man will soon fall for her. This bursar is too damned cunning.*" he mumbled and crept closer.

"I suspect you are very tired," the woman told the teacher for she suspected he was not interested in her, at least not tonight.

"You are quite right about that."

She nodded and fiddled with her bag, gazing wishfully at Mr Coker who now stood anticipating her departure. Embarrassed by his reticence, the woman decided to leave.

"I must leave now so that you will have your much-needed rest," the woman said.

"Thanks for your understanding," Mr Coker concluded as he gently closed the door after her and locked it.

The houseboy, squatting underneath the hibiscus bushes that lined the side of the principal's house, gave a big thumbs up when he saw the woman leaving. "*I hope you will continue to fail like tonight,*" he told himself.

Disenchanted over her utter rejection by Mr Coker, Martha went immediately to the bursar's house to update them on her futile attempt to ensnare the new principal.

"What happened?" The bursar asked when he saw the disillusioned face of her wife's friend.

"He did not even invite me to stay," the woman moaned.

"Son of a bitch," the bursar sneered impulsively.

"There is no need for you to be worried," the wife pleaded with the bursar. "Maybe he is just showing off since today is his first day in post. Some people like to take their time in a new job before doing anything and the way he speaks gives me the impression that he is a very meticulous person," the wife reasoned as she tried to calm her jittery husband down.

"Or maybe he is simply just tired from the long journey and he needs time to rest," Martha added.

"Let's hope so," the bursar said.

The fear that the new principal might be a difficult nut to crack was very much in play on his mind. He had been informed that the new principal had just been released from the maximum Pademba Prison. The bursar was in charge of five schools and was a central player in the clique that had enriched the family of the superintendent. The bursar was not sure whether the new principal would work in concert with him or go his own way. This worried him greatly.

In the morning, Mr Coker was awoken by the clanking of pans as the houseboy busied about the house cleaning the living and dining rooms.

"Good morning, sir. The water is ready in the bathroom," he told the Principal who had appeared at the window of the living room.

"Thank you."

He found the boy too frisky for his comfort and yet subservient, as well. Rather, he stole glances as the houseboy moved nimbly, from one corner of the house to the other, dusting, polishing and mopping the floors.

"Do you want me to heat the food the bursar's wife brought last night?"

"Just make me the same tea, like the one last night."

"What about the food, sir?"

"You can have it."

"Thank you very much sir," the houseboy said, inwardly pleased that the teacher was heeding his silent advice. He quickly prepared the tea and by the time Mr Coker came out of the bathroom, everything looked ready. Mr. Coker was impressed by the speed and attention with which the houseboy carried out his chores.

"I would like you to go and call the Vice Principal after eating your breakfast," he told the smiling houseboy.

"Yes, sir."

The houseboy took the lid off the pan containing the food from the bursar's wife. He was amazed by the content; lots of beef and other trimmings on top of the fried rice, boiled eggs planted on top of the rice, the usual insidious design used by the clever wife of the bursar to capture a new lover. The houseboy set about eating the food without heating it. He sat on the floor and quietly chewed every bone of the chicken. When he was full, he put the remainder of the food in a bowl and tucked it into his raffia bag.

*"My wife and children should share my good fortune,"* he told himself and dashed off to his house.

"Where did you get all this food from?" the houseboy's wife asked, quite puzzled by the quality and quantity of the food.

"The bursar's wife prepared it for the new principal, but he told me to take it. I think he is not comfortable eating the rice especially from people he'd just met for the first time."

"I am happy he did not touch the food because you cannot trust people anymore." the houseboy's wife said mockingly.

"Then let me throw the food away so that you and my children will not die if it is full of poison," he equally joked but as soon as he said this the wife quickly snatched the pan from the hands of her husband.

"If anything was put in it to win over the teacher, it would not affect any of us because it was not meant for us," the wife said, and she started picking the meat from the rice.

"Maybe it is poisoned," the houseboy continued trying to tease his wife.

"Then let me die, but I am going to eat and fill my belly. It has been a long time since I tasted such good food," the wife responded impulsively, laughing.

"If both of us die, who will take care of our children?" the houseboy continued in jest.

"May God forbid," the wife quickly said as she briskly warded off the statement by circling her head with her right hand. Mr Coker had already been sitting in the principal's office when the Vice Principal and the Bursar arrived.

"Good morning, sir," they greeted.

"Good morning, gentlemen," he responded with a smile. This put the Vice Principal at ease, because he knew they had taken a long time to react to the principal's call.

"We are sorry for coming late," the bursar said. "I had to take my daughter to the clinic this morning and the Vice Principal accompanied me," he continued to apologise for their lateness.

"I can understand, but please make sure you come to school on time when the school reopens next week. I do not have patience with people who come to work late," he warned both men. His face was stern and both men knew he meant his words.

Sewa Secondary School was the least developed school with the smallest enrolment in the whole of the Moyamba District. When the superintendent's elder brother opened the school, his main aim was to bolster Agriculture. Initially, everything worked according to plan and the school became famous for its agricultural programmes. With time, things began to deteriorate, and this was the main reason the teacher was hired to restore some glory to the school.

"We have to completely rebuild all the poultry and pig stalls in the farm," he told the Bursar and Vice Principal after inspecting the farm.

"The compound is covered in grass and it has to be brushed thoroughly before school reopens next week," he ordered.

"The brushing is done by the students when school reopens," the Vice Principal informed him.

"Things will be done differently this time. Labourers have to be hired to do the brushing," the teacher said. "Classes should start in earnest the first day of the school year. I have been told that students come late to school and leave before the end of the school day. This has greatly contributed to the indiscipline in the school and it has to stop if we want to develop standards in the school," Mr Coker ruled.

During his first staff meeting, Mr .Coker emphasised to the staff his zero tolerance for lateness by both the staff and students. However, most of them did not take him seriously, in particular they wondered how he would be able to manage such drastic changes without meeting the wrath of the students, most of whom were students expelled from other schools for being notorious trouble makers.

Within a very short period, the main building was completely rehabilitated and the whole compound brushed. The school now enjoyed a new look. On the first day of school, Mr.Coker went and stood in front of the main building and told all latecomers to stand under the sun. Moments later, he came outside and addressed all of them, and they were surprised by this new policy of the school.

"Any student who comes to school after 8am will not be allowed to enter any classroom. For you to be admitted, you must come with your parents to school."

The atmosphere became tense when Mr Coker made this pronouncement. Most students feared that by such action, their mischievous behaviour would be exposed to their parents.

"Today is the first day of school," one student vehemently protested.

"It does not matter whether it is the first day, or the last day. You have to be in school at 8am prompt," the Principal asserted. He left abruptly after making this strong statement, which gave no chance for the rowdy students to contend.

Among the students that were late for school and asked to bring along their parents to school the other day was a girl who was well known as a regular troublemaker. This morning she came in with a man whom she had asked to pretend to be her father. She knew the trouble she would be in if her parents knew about her mischievous actions in school. What she did not realise was that she had enlisted a retired schoolteacher who had a strong penchant for discipline. After all the parents and their children had gathered, Mr Coker explained to them the reason he had summoned them to the school. He explained the importance of education and encouraged them by telling them that teachers would only succeed if they had the cooperation of the parents. The speech was very touching, and the parents were moved by it because no other principal had asked them to take part in the running of the school activities of their children.

"You have our support," the ex-teacher whom the girl enlisted said. All the other parents shook their heads in agreement.

"I should have asked my teachers to flog the students in front of their fellow students, but that would not have the desired effect." The new Principal continued, "Not as much as when you do the flogging yourself, to demonstrate to your children that you are in agreement with the school, to bring back discipline in the school," the teacher told the parents.

"That is absolutely true Mr. Principal," the ex-teacher who now assumed the role of a self-ascribed spokesperson of the group shouted. Again, the rest of the parents nodded in agreement. The ex-teacher took the whip from the teacher and called the girl forward. He beat her thoroughly. All the other parents followed suit but not with the same level of ferocity that the ex-teacher had used to flog the girl.

The following day, all the teachers and all the students, with the exception of the perpetual truants, came to school on time. With that bold action on the second day of school, Mr Coker got a foothold on one of the major scourges of the school. The other problem was teachers flirting with the female students. During school functions, teachers openly seduced female students and it was rumoured that the former principal impregnated one of the students.

That day he called a meeting in which he discussed this serious issue with his staff.

"One thing I would not tolerate is teachers having intimate relationships with students," Mr Coker told his staff "Such actions will undermine discipline and academic performance. If we want this school to succeed, we the teachers should have a sense of rectitude in our profession," he continued and paused for responses.

Nobody contested his view, but the shuffling of feet and the twisting of faces underscored the fact that he had touched a sensitive nerve. The bursar wondered how the Principal would achieve his lofty goal when all the teachers were dating at least one girl in the school. After a brief and agonising silence, the Principal continued speaking.

"If you need any financial help, I prefer you come to me instead of going to borrow money from outsiders who would not keep your secrets." This pronouncement lightened the spirits of those teachers who for a very long time had been held hostage by the bursar who loaned them money and asked for huge interest in return. The bursar shifted to the edge of his wooden chair. He was visibly fuming.

"I asked the proprietor of the school to provide me with a revolving fund to help solve some of your immediate financial burdens and he has consented to help," the Principal said.

"Would there be any interest tagged·on these Loans?" one of the teachers asked.

"The school is not a bank," the Principal responded. All the staff members laughed except for the Bursar and the Vice Principal.

"Did I say anything funny?" he asked.

"No sir," a young teacher, whose facial expression was initially contentious when the teacher broached the topic, replied.

"One area we would like you to also help us with is that of rent. Since I joined the school, I have not been able to get a place for myself because most landlords refuse to have teachers as tenants" he continued.

"If you see any place that you want to rent, just come and tell me and I will contact the landlord. I am sure the owner of the property will be willing to rent if I stand as a surety."

All the teachers, with the exception of the Bursar and the Vice Principal, stood up and applauded their new leader, much to his surprise. He knew exactly where he was heading. His new policies were aimed at enhancing the living standards of the staff, boosting their morale and improving their outputs.

Over the following weeks, each staff member tried to do their best so that they would be recompensed by the Principal and this brought sanity that had mostly disappeared during the years of laissez-faire attitudes in the school.

# CHAPTER EIGHTEEN

"Brother Aruna, is that you?" One could hear Ya Feth's voice distinctly from the court-yard of Osman's compound as she spoke on the phone.

"When are you coming home to visit?" She continued to ask excitedly. Her elder brother had departed the shores of Sierra Leone over two decades ago. It had taken a long time since they spoke to each other. The indistinct voice on the phone could also be heard.

"Mother is dying slowly," she continued to shout, her laughter was dry and provocative to the neighbours.

"That's what you said a long time ago. Your long silence is not helping the situation. Do you want to visit after her death?" The rattling on the phone ceased for a while and soon it began again.

"How did you get my number after all these years?" Ya Feth continued with her queries. The rattling ceased again and the buzzing sound of the line dying could be heard. The phone had gone off. Shocked by this, her mind ran to Michael, the black American Peace Corp, who had once promised to help her find her brother. Michael became a family friend through her first son, Santigie. Teaching Michael at Saint Peter's catholic High School, Santigie was one of Michael's bright students. But soon, Santigie's grades began to go down and he would mostly be absent or come to school late. Other teachers also expressed the same sentiments about Santigie. Michael decided to intervene by visiting Santigie's parents to know what was going on. This evening, he met the two of them sitting outside the house.

"I am just very concerned about his recent attitude towards his schooling. Santigie hardly comes to school these days," Michael told Santigie's parents. "I just want to know if there's a problem," Michael continued.

"We noticed the difference too, "Osman responded, despondently. "He leaves here in his uniform. He comes home with watery and red eyes. He will simply go to his room without talking to anybody," Osman continued.

"Sometimes he sleeps in my classes, which is very unusual," Michael responded.

"He is a very good kid, but I noticed he is now hanging around with some bad kids in the neighbourhood. I tried talking to him about that, but he became confrontational, " Ya Feth explained amidst sobs.

"Is he taking something?" Michael asked.

"I think so," Osman said dejectedly.

"What have you done to help him?" Michael asked. His suspicion had been confirmed.

"I tried to, but his mother is always in the way."

"What can I do? He is my first son," the third wife said coyly.

"But love should have a boundary, especially when the welfare of the child is at stake," Michael tried to admonish her. "Both of you should work together if you want to help your child," Michael continued.

That was how Michael became known in Osman's household. He promised to help Santigie and he also promised to help the third wife find her brother who left for greener pastures in the white man's land a long time ago. And he kept his word. Aruna, the third wife's elder brother, finally visited the country during the festive month of December.

Before he left for the USA to undertake a post graduate degree in mechanical engineering at the university of Toledo, he became a very promising young man who graduated from Fourah Bay College (FBC) with a first class honours degree. At first, he remained in constant touch with the family back home. But as time went by, he stopped communicating.

"So you finally made up your mind to come and visit us?" Aruna's mother bitterly observed, her eyes welling.

"Sorry mom," Aruna said and embraced his mother. "Things have not been easy for me."

"But you should have called," Ya Safie, Aruna's mother, sharply interjected, "you got us all worried. In fact, we thought you were dead."

"You do not understand," Aruna said in a subdued tone.

"You do not understand what?" Aruna's mother thundered. "What about all those promises you made to help your sister and her children?"

"I need you to help me find out the reasons behind my constant misfortunes while in the white man's land," Aruna beseeched his mother and sister sadly, the third wife. "I think there's something wrong somewhere and that is what I have come to find out."

"We will get to the bottom of it," the mother said.

"I have seen only Santigie. Where are your other children?" Aruna asked her sister.

"Your other nephew, Kalilu, is in a boarding school in Makeni. So also, is Makalay, your niece," the third wife replied. "Both were causing too many problems for us, so Osman decided to send both of them away," she continued.

"What about Fatima?"

"She went to her mother's village to raise her only surviving son," the sister replied.

"Hmmm, this is scary. I heard she lost all her other children," Aruna said sadly.

Aruna's return to Sierra Leone was not marked by the usual exuberance received by other people from the diaspora who came to visit their hometowns. There were no expensive vehicles, no designer dresses, shoes or clothes. There were no gifts and money for his mother and siblings. Aruna looked gaunt and haggard. The town's people rumoured that he wasn't a true Johnnie Jess Cam or J. J. C, a name fondly attributed to people who had just arrived from abroad for holidays. Both mother and sister agreed that Aruna needed help. But Ya Baki felt happy with the conclusion that Aruna's trip to the "land of the plenty" was a complete disaster as she had desired for him.

"Did you see that fool who just arrived from the white man's land?" Ya Baki asked her friend when they met at the marketplace.

"I haven't seen him, but those who saw him told me he looked sickly and pitiful," the friend replied. "Did he come with any car?"

"What car?" The second wife asked sarcastically.

Both women laughed derisively, revelling in the misfortunes of Aruna.

"They haven't seen anything yet," Ya Baki bragged to her friend.

"I trust you," the friend said.

"How is your co-wife doing?"

"Don't mind that bitch," the friend replied, "she was growing some wings but the soothsayer cut them off. Thanks for introducing him to me. I don't know how to thank you," she continued.

"That's what true friendship is all about," Ya Baki replied and they both went their separate ways.

***

Due to the exigency surrounding Aruna's condition, both mother and sister decided to seek the help of a native doctor. After several investigations about reputable native doctors, they agreed on one, in the town of Kabala. The three of them left early in the morning for Kabala. When they arrived, Aruna explained everything that happened to him while in the white man's land. The native doctor threw several cowries on the floor and muttered incantations. He murmured for some time and proclaimed,

"There are evil forces in Osman's household that are behind all your problems."

"I knew it," the third wife shouted.

"But who is responsible?" Aruna asked.

The native doctor again cast the cowries on the floor and repeated his incantations. At last the native doctor declared, "the second wife of your husband is behind all this."

"I will kill that bastard of a witch," Aruna barked loudly.

"You do not have to do that," the native doctor cautioned.

"Then what do we do?" Both mother and sister asked in desperation.

"Leave that to me," the native doctor said calmly, "she will face equal punishment," he hastened to assure them. "I will show you all the sacrifices that you have to perform to solve Aruna's problems."

With the assurances of the native doctor, especially the retributive justice he promised to mete out on the second wife, the party left the town of Kabala with some Satisfaction.

# CHAPTER NINETEEN

The native healer was able to fully cure Salieu. He blossomed into a fine young man and his mother devoted her whole life in her quest to give him a very good education. She went back to Lunsar and there she struggled with her rice business. Her co-wives flourished in the town market where they built big stalls with the help, they received from Afiatu and her husband, Abess.

Fatima had to travel to the surrounding villages to buy rice and sometimes she went to faraway villages to buy rice. From the proceeds, she was able to send her son to a distinguished high school, with expensive boarding facilities. Salieu made many friends who came to his house on a daily basis. Fatima grew fond of one of them, a pretty young girl, called Alima, daughter of the section chief Pa Alimamy whom she hoped would become a good wife for her son

"You owe your mother too much," said one of Salieu's friends, after eating a meal.

"That is the privilege you enjoy when you are the only child," Salieu boasted and giggled.

Indeed, Salieu did enjoy the privileges of an over-indulged child. He was viewed by his friends as the new kid on the block. He wore the latest expensive shoes and costumes, which his mother bought willingly, just to keep him happy. After elementary school, Salieu moved on to one of the high schools in his town, but he opted to go to a prestigious school far away from home, Kolenten Secodary School, in Kambia

"I have been living in this town all my life and I want to go to a different place," he complained when his mother tried to persuade him to attend the local high school.

At the time, teenagers would normally move far away from home because it gave them the opportunity to share their experiences during holidays with other teenagers whose parents could not send them to boarding school. Those teenagers, whose parents hadn't the means to send them to schools outside the town, were often losers when it came to rivalry for the girls.

Salieu's high school was well known for academic excellence, and for sports. The man at the helm of things was a catholic priest who had a second-to-none desire for discipline and academic superiority. Being a spoilt child, Salieu suffered greatly during his first years for being lazy. He persistently earned the wrath of the reverend father, particularly for coming to school late.

"If you do not change your attitude, I will send you back home," the catholic father often warned Salieu when he caught him sleeping inside the dormitory during school hours. This time, he ran out of luck, and even when he tried to hide under the shimmering light, the principal saw him and dragged him from under his bed.

"I am not well and that is why I could not go to school today," Salieu said in self-defence.

"I have heard that several times from you students and this is the last time I am going to tolerate this nonsense from you," the catholic father replied sternly.

A week later, Salieu pulled the same stunt and the catholic father was less forgiving. He suspended him from school for three weeks, and from the boarding home, for the rest of the term.

Upon his return, Salieu reformed himself and took to playing football for the school. His academic performance also improved dramatically, and the catholic father used him as a poster boy to influence other students who had a turbulent beginning at the school.

"If Salieu can transform himself, any of you can," he frequently told stubborn students.

During holidays, when Fatima went in search of goods in the surrounding villages, she employed the services of Alima to help prepare food for the house. Many people knew she was nursing her for his son and Salieu no doubt had interest in Alima. He looked at her lustfully, sometimes dramatically drawing her attention, but the girl continued to do her job despite his cavalier attitude. Because of her polite and obsequious nature, Fatima soon began to see her as the daughter she never had. She showered her with kindness and affinity and Alima in turn looked up to her as the mother she never had. Like Salieu, she was the only daughter to her mother who died during childbirth but unlike other motherless children in polygamous homes, Alima was treated nicely by her stepmothers and siblings. This amicable relationship stemmed from her father, the section chief, who treated all his wives equally. Sibling rivalry did not exist in his household.

On this particular day, Alima busied herself preparing a lot of food. Salieu's friends were camping in the house for the important soccer game they had with Mamud's son.

"She will make a good wife," one of his friends commented.

"Cooking good food is not the only trait a man looks for in a wife?" Salieu bluffed to his friend.

"But she seems to get along with your mother pretty well because of her modesty and hard work and that is very important," the friend said. "If you have a wife with such good virtues and your mother likes her, then half of your marital problems are solved especially when you are the only son. Sometimes we tend to forget the feelings of our parents when we are looking for a wife and that can be dangerous because we need their blessings in making such an important decision," the friend further said.

"But I have to love the woman too," Salieu countered.

"That is right. But if the woman that you love does not get along with your mother, what do you do?" The friend insisted.

"Then I will marry another woman."

"If that one does not get along with your mother?"

"Then I will marry another."

"How many times are you willing to marry?"

"As long as it takes," Salieu said, smiling.

"It is better you do it right the first time, like the choice you have now," the friend said.

"Are you sure Alima did not bribe you to plead on her behalf?" Salieu joked.

"She did not. I am your friend and I know what is good for you."

They role played adult talks and they quickly shifted their discussion to the pending game when Alima entered the living room to collect the dirty bowls. All the friends were in awe of her beauty including Salieu whose indifference was noticeable by the way he looked at the girl and by the manner he handed his bowl to her. He was visibly besotted.

At the beginning of the football season, the team of Salieu and his friends, "THE PROMOTERS", bankrolled by Fatima, had many gifted players. But soon, most of these talented players went and joined the team of Mohamed, "THE YOUNG GENERATION". He was the son of Mamud, the biggest rice dealer in Lunsar, who wielded a lot of power in the community. In the town of Lunsar, there was an open proxy war between Abess, the Lebanese trader and Mamud, each trying to assert himself as the richest and most magnanimous. The popularity of Mamud began to soar when his son formed the soccer team with an excellent coach and sound finances. It remained undefeated in all its league games. The team of Salieu and his friends stayed in second place despite their financial difficulties.

"The game next week is crucial, and we must do something," one of the players suggested.

"We just have to practice harder," Salieu said.

"Even if we do that, we need outside assistance," the player continued.

"We do not have the money to hire mercenary players from the capital. We just have to move our game to another level if we want to win." Salieu continued.

"But there is a strong rumour that Mohamed has requested the help of some players from the capital and we will be humiliated if we do not seek help. We can ask your father's boss, Abess to help us. I am sure he will be willing to do so because of the rivalry between him and Mamud," the other player suggested.

"That is a good idea," Salieu agreed, "I will tell my mother to go and talk to Abess.

The next day, Fatima went to ask for money from Abess to support his son's team.

"The money you are asking for is too much," Abess told Fatima.

"It will be a loan from you," Fatima pleaded desperately with Abess.

With the loan from Abess, a star-studded team was quietly recruited from Freetown. According to the players, the game was too important to be left to chance. A day before the game, news reached Salieu's camp that the other team had solicited the help of a notorious witch doctor. "He would come to the field at night and burry things. During game time, he would stand at the back of the goalpost of the team he was protecting, and your team would not be able to score any goals," he told them.

"It depends on the strength of the other team," one religious teammate countered.

"When you believe in such nonsense then it will affect you," he continued.

"I do not believe in such things, but prevention is better than cure. Let us send somebody to the field the night before the game to watch for any unusual activities," another teammate suggested.

The night before the game, one avid supporter volunteered to police the field. He climbed one of the trees that lined the fence of the field. By mid-night, he saw two men digging the middle of the field and just after, they buried something. He could not recognise the men, but one was tall and deformed on the left leg, while the other walked with a hunch. When they left, the man went to the same spot, unearthed and urinated on the assorted items they had buried. The items included a white fowl with a severed head wrapped in a red cloth. There were also three red kola nuts. The supporter took the items to Salieu's camp after carefully covering up the spot again.

"I do not believe in such nonsense," the religious teammate protested.

"It is good that we have destroyed what they buried in the field, whether it is working, or not. It is better to be safe than sorry," the other teammate said.

"When you get to the field tomorrow, just roll over and play dead because you have destroyed their fetish," the religious teammate mocked.

On the day of the match, the tension in town was high among the opposing supporters, each predicting victory. Mamud's son's team was predicting a three-goal victory, corresponding to the three red kola nuts they believed their sorcerer had buried in the field. Both teams got to the field and the supporters were far more than the field could accommodate. The stewards, therefore, shut the gate well before the start of the match and most spectators clambered and sat on the fence, others, on trees, and still others peered through tiny holes on the fence.

Before the Referee blew his whistle, the spy that unearthed the items from the middle of the field saw the same two men behind the goal post of the opposing team.

"Those are the two guys I saw that night," he confirmed to the players of his team.

"They can stand there because they have the right," the religious teammate said and the conversation was dropped when the whistle was blown, alerting the teams to get ready.

During the game, the two linesmen, one on each side of the field, pushed the spectators off the pitch. Sometimes, supporters came right onto the turf when their team was in possession of the ball and threatening to score. The opposing team steadfastly defended, despite the barrage of attacks from the tactically astute team of Salieu. Many shots to the goal went off target and this surprised the players and their supporters.

"This is very unusual," Salieu complained to his teammates during the interval. After twenty minutes of play into the second half of the game, the supporters of Salieu's team went and attacked the two men they suspected of interfering with the game. A fight ensued and they succeeded in forcing both men out of the field. Moments later, the deadlock was broken. Four quick goals were scored in succession as the defence of the opposing team collapsed.

"Their eviction from the field had nothing to do with our victory," the religious team mate, who scored two of the goals, commented when the other team mates praised the men who had dragged the men suspected of using the charm behind the goal out of the field.

"We were able to score because they could no longer sustain the pressure of our attack."

After the game, the jubilant supporters of Salieu's team lifted shoulder high the hired players from the capital and danced with them. The crowd went to Mamud's street and sang provocative songs which resulted in a fight between supporters of the two teams.

They sang about the mysterious and a dark cloud that hung over the origin of Mamud's wealth. There were variations to the story but the one mostly sung about was about diamonds. When Mamud was a young man, he left his farming village and went to the diamond rich area of Kono. It was a common practice at the time for young men to leave their poor farming villages and go in search of quick wealth.

Because of his determination, Mamud soon gained the trust of his Lebanese master who made him one of his drivers. It was rumoured that during one of their diamond trips, Mamud attacked his boss, took the diamond and set the car on fire. He inflicted some injuries on his body and reported they had a gruesome accident and their car got ablaze. Later, the charred body of the Lebanese was found in the burnt car. Initially, Mamud was arrested, but later released because there was no corroborating evidence that the accident was staged. However, other people suspected that he bribed his way out of custody. Others argued that his release was retributive justice for the Lebanese merchant who cheated his employees by paying them pittances. Shortly after that incident, Mamud returned to his village and embarked on large scale farming. Despite his success in farming, some begrudged him for what they considered as ill-gotten wealth. Later, he relocated to Lunsar after having a bitter experience with his first wife who made him the laughingstock of the village when she betrayed his trust by bringing a village lout into their matrimonial bedroom. They sang all this in their songs.

# CHAPTER TWENTY

With the support of his mother, Salieu entered Fourah Bay College (FBC) where he studied History. During his time at the university, many of the facilities enjoyed by past students were suspended, or minimised due to the austerity measures taken by the government. The cafeteria system was abolished, and students had to cook their own meals.

Still worse, Salieu didn't make the grade to earn him a scholarship. His mother footed the bills for his college education. He also received help from Fanta, the daughter of Mamud, whom he had started dating despite the obvious disapproval of his mother.

"Alima is a nice girl and I do not know why you recently don't like her," said Fatima.

"Every young man in this town is dying to date Fanta. She is helping me a lot and you know your business is not doing well as before," Salieu had pleaded with his mother.

"All I am saying is that Alima is a good woman and everybody in this neighbourhood is saying that. You know Fanta feels too good of herself because of the wealth of his father. You know quite well that I do not have a daughter and if you have a woman like Alima as your wife, she will become the daughter I never had," Fatima reasoned with her son.

"I would like you to give Fanta a chance. Once you come close to her, you will realise that she is a very nice woman," Salieu assured his mother.

"My son," Fatima called softly, "Alima will be a better wife."

"If she is all that bad, why is it that so many of my friends want to marry her? I think she has some good qualities in her and she is very beautiful."

From his argument, Fatima knew it would be a futile attempt to try to convince her son; he seemed to have made up his mind to continue his relationship with Fanta. Not wanting to hurt him further, she reduced her reproach of Fanta but her inner reservations remained unchanged. What worried her most was the means her father used to make money. For some time now, he had monopolised the rice business as the Rice Marketing Board made him the sole distributor of rice in the whole of the region. He hoarded the supply and created artificial scarcity, making small-scale traders like her to run out of business. He made money and bought houses from distressed people at very low prices. He had houses in Freetown, some he sold at huge prices, others he rented out. People believed that he owned over twenty houses in Freetown.

To strengthen his position further, Mamud got into the politics of Lunsar and he became the king maker. The Member of Parliament for Lunsar had been in parliament for many years, but he proved to be very unproductive. A notorious backbencher who had never participated in parliamentary discussions. In fact, members of his constituency had nick-named him *"I concur"* to remind him of his only contribution in parliament. Because of his inability to advance the causes of Lunsar, the people became fed up with him and decided they would vote him out at the next general election. They had chosen a more charismatic candidate, but this choice did not sit well with Mamud who was in full support of the Member of Parliament.

"You do not have to worry about anything," Mamud reassured the worried Member of Parliament.

"But the people were very determined, this time, to vote for another candidate."

"What you have to understand is that my friend, Adnan, the wealthy businessman is on your side. He has assured me that he will do everything possible for you to be re-elected. It is important to be connected with people that matter in the society," Mamud assured the already distraught MP.

The mention of Adnan's name calmed the MP who knew the support of Mamud alone wasn't enough to thwart the determination of the people of Lunsar. Like Mamud, Adnan used deceptive tactics and shrewd business practices to amass a lot of wealth in the diamond business. Within a short period of time, he became a force to reckon with in the business circles. He became a friend of the president and so had the privilege to attend cabinet meetings where important matters affecting the state were being discussed. With such a powerful concession, the fate of most of the ministers was in his hands. He was put in charge of the diamond mining company, Sierra Leone Selection Trust (SLST) and his influence multiplied.

During elections, he made sure that only those people whose candidacy he approved got elected to parliament through a sham "unopposed system" perpetrated through thuggery. One good candidate whom Adnan didn't approve was the one the people of Lunsar wanted to represent them in parliament. He saw him as being instrumental in mobilising the indigenes of Lunsar who chased him out when the beating of his nanny resulted in her death.

"Not even over my dead body will that arrogant man become the MP for Lunsar," Adnan had sworn to Mamud.

"Even if all the people of Lunsar are on his side, he will not represent this constituency," he continued. "But the people are determined this time," the nervous MP said.

"What the people want is irrelevant as long as I do not endorse it," he'd boasted.

And that was exactly what happened. On the day of the election, the town of Lunsar got swamped with thugs who blocked the road that led to Portloko, the district headquarters where the nominations were made. The contender and some of his die-hard supporters were rounded up and locked in the police station. They were released the next day, immediately after all the nominations had been completed and the winners declared. The incumbent MP was re-elected unopposed and sent to parliament for another five-year term. These highhanded brutal tactics were the order of the day in the political system of Sierra Leone, which had left many people disillusioned about the direction the politics of the country was heading. Unemployment, high cost of living and brutality became rife and many people, particularly the youth, became bitter.

Salieu got a teaching job at the Guadalupe Secondary School for Girls in Lunsar, built by the Catholic missionaries. This job gave him the opportunity to stay close to home that helped him to take care of his mother whose health was now deteriorating. The lump the healer told her about had developed into a lymphedema on her leg. Since it was painless, only Salieu knew about it. His salary could not sustain them all and so he could not afford to take her to the hospital. The situation became worse when Fanta's father suffered a stroke and later died. The sibling rivalry for the possession of the dead man's wealth polarised the entire family.

Mamud had six wives and twenty-six children. Some of the children were not old enough to fight for their rightful inheritance and most were left out when the properties were shared. Fanta and her three brothers and two sisters were given one of the houses in Freetown, which their mother rented to upkeep them. The two eldest sons of Mamud managed the family business.

The death of Mamud and the decline of the family business brought hardship to

Fanta and her other siblings. She could not continue with her schooling. She later succumbed to Salieu's pressure and got married to him. But, as always, Fanta disliked Fatima, now her mother-in-law. In most cases, her mother would come over to help her rein insults on the defenceless woman.

"My daughter will stay here with your son whether you like it or not. I know you did not like my daughter from the very first day she met with your son, but you will not succeed because she is now his wife. The woman you are preparing for Salieu will have to look for another man," Fanta's mother accosted Fatima. In all this, Salieu's interventions, most times coming from work, were lame.

Three weeks later, things worsened. Salieu left for Portloko to invigilate the GCE exams and Fanta gave her mother-in-law rice without soup.

"Where is the soup for the rice?" She asked Fanta who was sitting on the veranda gazing blankly into the street.

"Your son did not give me any money for the soup. Do you want me to cut my fingers and cook soup for you? You must talk to him to stop wasting his money in the street with other women," Fanta told Fatima.

"Why did you not ask me to give you money for the soup this morning?" Fatima asked.

"Give the money to your son when he comes back. You think I do not know what you and your son are up to?"

"What are you talking about?" Fatima asked, looking dazedly at her daughter-in-law, bewildered by the sudden accusation.

"You know what I am talking about. But let me assure you that your plans will fail," Fanta replied with a hiss.

"You must realise that I am older than your mother. Please be respectful to me if not for being your mother-in-law, but someone old enough to be your grandmother," Fatima said.

"Even if you are old as the cotton tree in Freetown, it is not my business," Fanta sharply retorted with rolling eyes.

"Please watch your mouth, young woman," Fatima snapped.

"You cannot do anything to me," Fanta barked.

"I will wait for my son's return then I will explain to him how you have continued to be rude to me."

"He cannot do anything to me," Fanta responded with a snap of the fingers.

Stunned by her reply, Fatima went to Alima'a house and asked her to come and help her prepare some soup for the rice. Without asking any question, Alima dressed and came back with Fatima.

"What do you think you are doing?" Fanta asked Alima who was busy stoking the fire.

"I am cooking some soup for Fatima," Alima calmly replied.

"If you want to cook for her, you can do it in your own house but not here."

"She asked me to do the cooking here," Alima said.

"I do not care what she told you. All I am saying is that you cannot cook in this house. If you think that by doing this Salieu will marry you? You are making a big mistake," Fanta spoke in a loud tone that caught the attention of Fatima.

"What is the matter?" Fatima asked Alima who was shocked by her belligerent tone.

"She told me I cannot cook in this kitchen. If I want to cook for Salieu, I have to do it in my house," Alima said.

"She does not have any right to stop you from cooking in this house that I built with my own money," Fatima told Alima.

"Continue with the cooking and let me see what she is going …"

Before Fatima could finish her statement, Fanta stormed into the kitchen and threw water into the fire Alima was stoking and threw the pot outside with its contents strewn all over the kitchen floor. The dog, lying longingly at the far corner of the kitchen, sprang to his feet and started swallowing some of the fish. Fanta hit him mercilessly with a firewood stick.

"You don't have to eat that fish," she screamed at the dog as it ran outside crying painfully from the unexpected vicious attack from his owner.

"Why did you do that?" Fatima asked, blocking the entrance to the kitchen.

Without uttering any word, Fanta pushed her mother-in-law out of the way. Fatima stumbled onto the bundles of firewood kept on the side of the kitchen.

"Next time you will not stand on my way," Fanta yelled.

"You do not have any right to push her," Alima confronted Fanta.

"Don't you know that this is the mother of your husband?" She continued to reproach.

"Please mind your own business," Fanta replied.

"If you want to be part of this fight, just continue putting your mouth into our affair then you will see what will happen to you. You man snatcher. Even if you come here every day and cook, Salieu will never marry you," Fanta continued seething with anger.

The loud cries of Fatima brought some neighbours to the scene. She showed them the bruises on both of her hands.

"What have I done to deserve this?" Fatima asked the neighbours repeatedly who could not understand how a daughter-in-law would behave so badly to her mother-in-law. Feeling a deep sense of shame, Fatima left the scene and bolted herself in her room. The empathies expressed by the neighbours were too much burden for her to handle.

"What is the world coming to?" One old man asked with a gaping mouth.

"During our time, a daughter-in-law could not even look at her mother-in-law in the face. I think the world is coming to an end," the old man continued, covering his mouth with his left hand, a bit ashamed by his almost tainted toothless mouth.

The incident became the topic of discussion in the neighbourhood; and many were sure Salieu would get rid of Fanta when he returned from his trip.

"Your wife nearly killed me when you left," Fatima told her son the moment he entered the house.

"Look at the bruises on my hand. She pushed me towards the firewoods. Yesterday was cursing, today is pushing, what will happen tomorrow?"

"Yayo, you should realise that she becomes easily upset these days," Salieu told her mother.

"What do you mean?" Fatima asked, eyes glaring with frustration.

"She is three months pregnant and this is making her get angry easily," Salieu informed his mother whose face had eased.

"Since this is our first child, I did not want to tell you, because I know you will tell other people and we wanted to keep it a secret until the right time."

Fatima stood motionless, overwhelmed by the news of the pregnancy of the woman that had tormented her all this time. Inside her, a feeling of joy for the birth of her first grandchild overcame the anger that had consumed her ever since Fanta moved into her house.

"I will tell her to come and apologise to you for her misbehaviour," Salieu finally told her mother who had not uttered a single word since he broke the news to her.

"She does not need to apologise," Fatima said.

"Are you saying you have forgiven her?"

"I am just so happy at the moment because of what you told me. I have been waiting for a long time for the day when I would hold my grandchild. I hope it is going to be a girl," Fatima told her son.

The news about the pregnancy brought some tranquility in the home. Fatima became amenable to Fanta's occasional outbursts as well as her lazy behaviour, which became a major source of their frequent quarrels.

"You look happy this morning," a woman selling fish at the market commented when she heard Fatima singing.

"My daughter-in-law is pregnant, and I am practicing the songs I have to sing to my grandchild," Fatima said.

"Is this your first grandchild?"

"Yes."

"I can understand. I was in the same mood when I learned that my daughter was pregnant. In fact, I had to move to her house three months before the baby was due and I stayed there for a whole year helping her with the baby," the woman said.

"My daughter-in-law stays with me," Fatima said.

"That makes it much easier for you. I had to travel back and forth to go and play with my grandchildren. Take one more heap of fish as my gift to the expectant mother," the woman told Fatima.

"Thanks very much."

Impressed by the kindness of the total stranger, Fatima left the market humming fecklessly the song about the wicked wife who never allowed her mother-in-law to play with her grandchild. Fanta and Salieu were still in bed after Fatima had prepared the soup. She went and gently knocked on the door.

"Who is it?" Salieu asked, thinking that one of his students had come to ask him for help, as they usually did, early in the morning.

"I have prepared some soup for Fanta." Fatima replied.

"It is good for her to drink soup early in the morning. That will help to keep her alert for the rest of the day," she continued.

Salieu opened the door and took the soup.

"It smells good." Salieu complimented his mother who gave a broad smile in response. "Did she sleep well last night?" Fatima asked with a worried look on her face.

"Yes, she did," said Salieu and mentioned a farewell to her mother before closing the room.

"Your mother has been very nice to me of late," Fanta told her husband.

"Ever since I told her about the pregnancy, all the anger she had for you just disappeared. She is very excited about the baby."

"Your mother has changed but you have not. You will soon be a father, and this means new responsibilities. The time you spent playing that foolish game of draught with your friends does not help you," Fanta scolded her husband.

"This is the reason why we had that argument last night. You are always accusing me of one thing and another. If I am not playing my foolish game, I am chasing married women or my students."

"You always get angry when I tell you the truth," Fanta replied.

"What do you want me to do after school? I do not drink or smoke. Things are difficult these days and the only way to relieve myself from stress is to go and play draught with my friends."

"Everybody knows things are difficult, but you have to try other things. My father never went to college, but he was successful out of the sheer will to succeed."

"I have looked for another job but there is none. I have to be thankful at least I have a job," Salieu tried to defend himself.

"This government has disappointed the youth of this country. I am a university graduate but look at the life of poverty we are living. I cannot even afford to eat a decent meal. My greatest worry at the moment is how am going to provide for my child."

"Are you expecting the government to do everything for you?" Fanta scolded her husband.

"I am not saying that."

"Then stop being lazy," Fatima said angrily, "Try doing something else."

"Like what? I do not have the starting capital to do business."

"There are many schools in town. You can start by organising tutorial classes for students taking the GCE exams. I am sure they will come to your review classes because of the high respect they have for you."

"Students do not have the money to pay for extra classes."

"But have you tried it?" Fanta asked, disappointed that her husband was always wary to try new things.

"Apart from the review classes, you can also make pamphlets and sell to the students."

"I have thought of that before, but the returns are just too small compared to the energy spent to prepare the pamphlets. You are bringing all these ideas because you do not want to pressure your brother to help me get a better job that will help to change our living conditions," Salieu complained.

"You know quite well that brother of mine is not interested in helping his half brothers or sisters. I have spoken to him several times about your request, but I have not received any positive response from him."

"Just continue to put pressure on him," Salieu pleaded.

"You are always asking me to put pressure on my elder brother. Your stepmothers and some of your siblings are successful. Why don't you ask them?"

"You pretend as if you do not know what has happened between my mother and her mates. Apart from driving her from the house they succeeded in poisoning the minds of their children against us. I prefer to die in poverty than ask any help from them because of what they did to my mother. I will continue to try my own way until I get a better job."

"But you have tried for a long time now without any success. How long are you going to try?" Fanta asked sarcastically.

"As long as it takes," Salieu crowed dismissively.

"Please make sure you drink the soup before it gets cold," Fatima shouted from the adjacent room, tired of eavesdropping on the wrangling between Salieu and his pregnant, feisty, wife.

Throughout the pregnancy, Fatima gave unconditional, emotional and physical support to her daughter-in-law. On the night Fanta started experiencing labor pains, she was instrumental in minimising the pangs of childbirth by giving her the same concoctions that Ya Yanoh had given to her in the early hours of the morning that stopped the bleedings and the massive pain she was experiencing. After that horrible experience, she asked the midwife to show her how to prepare that mixture. A week before Fanta started experiencing her labor pains, Fatima had already prepared the lotion and kept it under her bed in readiness for the momentous day. The potion was magical in its effect and it allowed Fanta to have a quick delivery.

"The medicine Fatima gave me helped a lot," Fanta told her mother who was busy washing the baby.

"I am sorry I could not be here," the mother replied.

"The baby looks just like its dad. I only hope he will not be as lazy as him," the mother added with a frowned face.

"This is not the right time," Fanta pleaded with her mother who lately despised Salieu because of his non-aggressive nature.

"You very much supported this relationship in the beginning and now you are criticising him," she added.

"I do not want you to defend his laziness. Some of his friends they graduated from university are doing well because of their aggressive nature. Your husband prefers to go and play draught every evening instead of finding something to do," the mother complained bitterly.

"I have already spoken to him about that," Fanta told her mother.

"What was his response?" the mother asked as Fanta went outside to throw the water that she had used to wash the baby. The splash of water landed on the dog that was lying longingly on the veranda floor. The dog stood up and shook himself several times before finding another spot on the veranda where he squatted.

Fanta replied to her mother when she entered the room,

"He promised to find a better job…"

"I have heard that before," the mother sharply interjected before her daughter could finish.

"Please turn down the volume of that old radio. Its voice is too harsh for the baby."

"I know you want to tell me that it is the same radio I bought for him while he was in college," Fanta said bitterly.

"What else in this room that is not yours?" The mother asked.

"The chairs, the bed and even the bed sheets are the same ones that you bought since he was in college. This man has not bought anything new since you came to this house. What type of husband is this? He cannot even buy enough things for the baby's needs."

"Teachers are poorly paid." Fanta tried to defend her deficient husband.

"The fact of the matter is that he lacks initiative. That is plain and simple," the mother continued her assault on her son-in-law.

Early in the morning, Fatima got up and prepared some food for the lactating mother. Since Fanta's mother arrived, she had taken over the task of washing the baby every morning. Fatima only had limited access to the baby, and this didn't sit well with her. But, she continued to play her usual role of preparing food in the morning.

"You have to move to my house with the baby," Fanta's mother said after looking at the food Fatima prepared.

"You need good food as a suckling mother. Apart from that, this place is too crowded for the baby. It is very dangerous for three of you to share the same bed. I will tell your husband when he returns from work."

Fatima was deeply hurt by the constant tongue lashing of Fanta's mother of her son. Such harsh recriminations, she thought, were not necessary. Her son was not a loser as Fanta's mother had labeled him. He went to the university and completed his studies but could not earn enough money to take care of her or his family.

"It is not nice to blame my son," she told herself. But what put her sufferance to the brink was when she heard Fanta's mother suggesting to her daughter to go and stay with her with her grandchild. She knew such a move, if endorsed by his son, would take the baby away from her.

That day, Salieu came home late and Fanta's mother had left for her house.

"Your mother-in-law is planning to take your daughter and your wife to her house," Fatima complained to her son the moment he entered the house.

"Nobody told me anything about that," Salieu said.

"I am telling you what I heard from her this morning when you left for work," Fatima said invigoratingly, emphasising to her son the implication of such a move.

"I will talk to her tomorrow morning when she comes," Salieu said lamely without looking at his mother. He knew she wanted an immediate affirmative answer, which he was not prepared to give at the moment. This move by him left her mother confused, not knowing whether her son would yield to the outlandish plan of her nagging mother–in-law or not.

This feeling of anxiety kept her awake for most part of the night. She painfully drifted into sleep but was awoken in the early hours of the morning by the loud, strident, voice of Fanta's mother.

"She has to move to my house because I cannot continue to come here every day. My mother is sick, and I also want to take care of her," Fanta's mother protested to Salieu. The emphasis with which she spoke showed she was serious. When her husband was alive, many of the employees were averse to her tempestuous character.

"I think my mother would like to take care of her grandchild," Salieu said.

"She is my grandchild too," Fanta's mother snapped.

"All Salieu is saying is that I can be of help since you have to take care of your mother and will not be able to come here every day," Fatima came to the defense of her son.

"When you had your son, did you not go to your mother's village to raise him?" Fanta's mother asked.

"The circumstances were different," Fatima said.

"What makes them different?" Fanta's mother asked sharply.

"I took him to the village to save his life," Fatima responded.

"I am taking the baby to my house to save his life too. How can you expect my daughter to share this tiny bed with her husband and my grandchild? When he is man enough to buy a new bed that is big enough for the three of them, then my daughter and grandchild will return," Fanta's mother responded, picking things and shoving them into her bag.

"You have to understand our situation," Fatima said, her lips quivering, "you have other grandchildren to play with and you are taking the only one I have," she continued.

"If you want her to stay, then you can go and get a new bed," Fanta's mother mocked.

She knew that Fatima and her son were cash strapped.

"I am waiting for your response," Fanta's mother continued to mock.

Fatima was embarrassed by the ineffectual attitude of her son. As the father, she had expected him to take charge of the situation by forcefully countering the unreasonable demands of his arrogant mother-in-law.

"I am only a helpless grandmother," she told herself and left the room disconsolately.

The moment his mother left, Salieu went to the inner section of the room and put on his clothes. He groped underneath his bed for his only pair of black shoes, quickly applied Kiwi Polish on them and left the room in a hurry.

"The white man that made those shoes should be given credit," Fanta's mother mocked again.

"Please stop mother. You have embarrassed him enough," Fanta came to the defense of her husband.

"I do not want to hear a word from you," Fanta's mother roared.

"You should be ashamed of yourself for choosing such a husband. There are many good homes in this town to choose a husband from, but you have decided to end up in this house where poverty says good morning at the first cock crow. Your father must be turning in his grave at this time with disappointment," the mother bitterly complained.

"You have to be patient with him," Fanta continued to plead with her mother.

"I have been patient enough. Since his early years in college, I have been helping him. But your husband is too lazy. His friends are aggressive enough to have made use of their lives without anybody helping them," the mother responded angrily.

After several rebukes, Fanta yielded to the demands of her mother. She left the house with her immediately after washing the baby. Fatima made a last-ditch effort to persuade Fanta not to leave, but she could not go against the wishes of her mother who was bent on achieving her desired goal of putting an end to a relationship she had come to despise of late.

# CHAPTER TWENTY ONE

Fatima wept bitterly when her grandchild was taken away. The anguish of not being able to wash and cuddle the baby was too much to bear. Her depression reached a state that she suffered a broken heart. Her eyes became sunken for lack of sleep.

"I wish I had not left the village," Fatima told herself. *I wish I had allowed the teacher into my life*, she pondered

Because Fatima wanted to prove her virtuousness to her husband, and because she didn't want to be the one responsible for the breakdown of her marriage, for she knew very well that was what people would say even when they were aware of what Osman and his wives had done to her, Fatima had long asked Mr Coker to stop visiting. But he had been very helpful to Salieu when he was at university. Fatima now regretted this, for Osman had not changed his attitude toward her.

"You look so sick. What's wrong with you?" Alima asked Fatima when she came to her house during her routine visits.

"My grandchild has been taken away by Fanta's mother," Fatima said wistfully.

"Did Fanta have a fight with your son?" Alima asked again.

"No. She said the bed is too small for all of them to sleep in. She will only bring the baby back after my son has bought a bigger bed," Fatima explained, her body trembling.

"She knows my son cannot afford to buy the bed and she used it as an excuse to take the baby away from us."

"I think it is not right for Fanta to leave the house because of the bed," said Alima.

"When I was a child, my stepmother had only one bed and all of us, six in number, lived in that room," Fatima responded.

"What did your son do?"

"He went to the police and reported the matter, but he was referred to the social services. He is going there tomorrow"

"I think that is the right thing to do," said Alima.

Salieu arrived at the social services early on Friday morning. On the door, the working hours were boldly written:

MONDAY TO FRIDAY: 8AM - 4PM.

He glanced at his watch; it was 7:30 am.

"Thank God, I have only thirty minutes to wait," he told himself. Minutes later, he heard someone shout out:

"Good, boiled, cassava and soup for your breakfast."

It was a woman from a distance, and she was coming his end. When she came close, she raised her voice a little, looking at Salieu expectantly. Realising he had not eaten any breakfast, Salieu beckoned the woman to come.

"This cassava is good," the woman continued with her pitch.

"Let me try a little and see if what you are saying is true," he requested.

"How much do you want?" The woman asked with a quizzical look.

"Just one chunk for a trial."

"Are you a teacher?" the woman asked.

"Yes I am."

"Then I can understand," the woman replied scornfully.

"Apart from our salary, which is very small, we do not have anywhere to steal like other people," Salieu defended, trying to assert himself once again.

"I used to sell at the elementary school, but the teachers nearly run me out of business. They borrowed and borrowed and never paid back," the woman protested.

"The cassava is good," Salieu said, "I need some more," he continued with a smile.

He bought four more chunks, scooped a cup of water from the bucket a girl was carrying on her head and gulped the water down.

"Is she your daughter?" He asked.

"Yes," the woman replied, breaking the cassava into pieces and placing them on the rubber plate.

"Why is she not in school?" Salieu asked.

"They don't have school today," the woman said and poured soup over the lumps.

"It's nice that your daughter is helping you," he said, not sure the woman had told him the truth.

"I want to be a good housewife. Her father and I were here at the social services two weeks ago because he does not want to give us money. He left me with her when she was just six months and married another woman," the woman explained and handed the plate to Salieu.

"I also have a problem with my wife and mother-in-law. They took my daughter without my permission and I want the social services to help me," Salieu said, cutting a piece of the cassava and shoving it into his mouth.

"I wish you good luck," the woman responded as if trying to warn him against something.

"What do you mean?" Salieu asked, his spoon raised halfway to his mouth. The woman lifted the bowl to her head, muttered a statement and left with her daughter trailing behind. She continued her hollering along the street. By the time Salieu looked at his watch, it was 9am and the doors of the social services were still locked. Disappointed by the apathy of government workers, he made up his mind to leave and come back the next day. As he got up to leave, a woman, dressed in white, approached. She held a bag and swayed from side to side as she walked, her laborious gait dictating her weighty body.

"Good morning," she greeted politely.

"I am sorry for coming late. I had to take care of some personal business. Are you the only person here?"

"Yes." Salieu answered.

"This is the reason why I hate coming here in the morning." the woman grumbled.

"But the time written on the door is 8am-4pm, Monday through Friday," Salieu said with an air of seriousness.

"I have not been paid for six months and I have to do other things to survive," the woman replied as she opened the door casually.

There was drabness in the room, and this made Salieu to sneeze. The social worker quickly opened the windows and parted the curtains. The room had one big table and three long benches that lined the sides that could sit up to ten people. There were also four small wooden chairs in front of the table and a bigger one on the back, which made a crunching sound when the fat woman slumped into it. There was a small bundle of papers in a tray that suggested to Salieu that people seldom visited the place.

"Please sit down. Welcome to the social services. My name is Sento and what can I do for you today?" The social worker sounded businesslike, showing no qualms over the dilapidated condition of the place.

"My wife took our daughter to her mother's place without my consent," he explained.

"Did you talk to your mother-in-law about the matter?" the woman asked.

"She was the one that forced her daughter to make the horrible decision of taking the baby to her house because I have a small bed that is not spacious enough for the three of us."

"How old is the baby?"

"She is three weeks old."

"If that is the case, she is right. Many horrible accidents have occurred when young babies are accidentally squeezed to death by their parents while sleeping. To solve the problem, you can buy a bigger bed or a crib for the baby," the social worker advised.

"I do not think the bed is the issue. The woman hates me," Salieu said and looked at the woman pensively.

"Do you have the money to buy the crib?"

Salieu scratched his head several times as if looking for the proper answer to give before answering.

"I do not have the money at the moment that is why I came to the social services for help."

"Our office does not receive any funding from the government. The social services have been neglected by the government and the office is purely symbolic. My role here is primarily advisory. What is the name of your mother-in-law?"

"Her name is Safiatu."

"One of the widows of Mamud?" The woman asked.

"That is she, that wicked woman," Salieu Said and gritted his teeth.

"I know the woman very well. You have to swallow your pride and find some elders to talk to her. That is the only way that will help to soften her stance. If we were properly funded, I would have sent a request to my boss for a new crib for your baby."

Salieu now put into perspective the words of the woman selling the boiled cassava and soup: "I wish you good luck." Caught in what seemed like an unsolvable problem, Salieu left the office of social services. As he walked home, the words of the social services woman hammered in his head. The more he thought about the notion of approaching his mother-in-law, the more he became downhearted.

He knew quite well the growing chord of deep animosity his mother-in-law harboured in her for him only because he was unable to improve the welfare of her daughter. She did not even want to see him lately and her breathtaking hatred of him was further manifested in the disparaging way she spoke to him. He now felt more despondent going back home than when he had come to the social services. From a distance, he could see his mother standing on the veranda. She wore an ever-ready worried face.

"Any luck?" Fatima asked when Salieu approached, but the tauten face of her son told the whole story.

"I was able to sell the Lappa this morning, but I don't think it is enough money to by the bed," Fatima informed her son.

"I do not think buying the bed will solve the problem. She only used it as an excuse to take the baby away. The social worker advised that we find some elders to talk to her. I think that will soften her position against me," Salieu explained.

"I think Pa Alimamy will be of help. We can use the money I got from the Lappa to ask Pa Alimamy to call some elders to go with us," Fatima suggested.

"I think that is a good idea."

Pa Alimamy had been a section chief even before Salieu was born. Many people admired the way he ran his household. With four wives, one would have expected his compound to be a hot bed for quarrels, but the relatively dignified atmosphere in his compound was uncharacteristic of men with many wives, and that was one of the main reasons he was appointed section chief by the paramount chief.

"I think you are the only person that will be able to help us," Fatima told Pa Alimamy after she had explained the matter to him.

"I will do my best. I do not need any money from you because I see Salieu as my son," he told Fatima when she made to give him money.

Instead of sending an emissary, which was the tradition, Pa Alimamy went to the house of Fanta's mother himself early the next morning. The children were sweeping the compound and Fanta's mother was seated on a stool strewing rice crumbs for her chickens. She held a long stick in her left hand, which she used to drive away one of the cocks tormenting the others.

"Stop sweeping," Fanta's mother yelled at the little girl who was still sweeping when Pa Alimamy entered the compound. She rose from her seat and reverently greeted the section chief.

"What a surprise visit," she said.

"That means the matter is serious," Pa Alimamy said jokingly.

"Have I committed any crime?" Fanta's mother asked smiling.

"If you commit any crime, I do not have to come to you," the section chief said.

"Then it means you have only come to pay me a visit so early in the morning."

"The best time to pay somebody a visit that you need help from is early in the morning, when all the evil spirits are still sleeping," said Pa Alimamy.

The section chief and Fanta's mother exchanged further pleasantries until he felt comfortable to talk about his mission to her.

"It is only a man like you that will talk to me about that foolish Salieu who thinks to be a man is simply putting on your pants," Fanta's mother said, her face contorted.

"I have daughters too and I know how painful it is when you have a lazy son-in-law," the section chief tried to soothe Fanta's mother.

"I would like you and your daughter to come to my compound this evening so that we can try and settle the matter. His mother came to me yesterday and asked me to help them on this."

"You are our section chief. I cannot deny your request no matter how mad I am. We will be there this evening," Fanta's mother said.

"Thank you very much for giving me the chance to try and solve the problem between you and your son-in-law." Pa Alimamy said goodbye and left.

Salieu and his mother were the first to arrive at the section chief's house. When Fanta and her mother came, they simultaneously greeted them but the response from the mother was halfhearted. The stern look in her face portended trouble. She was holding the baby and when Salieu came close to play with the child, his hand was waved off. He went back and sat dejectedly on his seat. Sensing the tension, the section chief decided to go straight to the heart of the matter after greeting both parties. He directed his remarks to Salieu.

"I have not come to ask questions between you and your mother-in-law. It is against tradition. She is angry because she felt you have not made enough efforts to better yourself."

"I have been trying but I have not been fortunate," Salieu calmly responded. But before he could continue, his mother-in-law interjected.

"Not when you spend most of your time playing draught and chasing other women."

"I want to apologise on his behalf," Fatima said.

"You are equally responsible for his actions. You showed him too much love. You never allowed him to grow up, you provide everything for him," Fanta's mother complained.

"You cannot blame me for doing that. He is my only child," Fatima said, tears streaming down her face. She raised the loose end of her Lappa and wiped her wet face.

"And this is the result. A man who cannot do anything for himself." Salieu shifted in his seat and adjusted his posture.

"What would you like to say to your mother-in-law?" The section chief intervened. It was a question for Salieu, but the section chief intended it to save him from the onslaught of the mother-in-law.

"I just want her to give me one more chance. A friend of mine we went to the university together has promised to help me. I am very hopeful of his promise this time around," Salieu explained.

Fanta looked at her husband with unflinching rage. She rolled her eyes several times at him and quickly adjusted her Lappa parting between her legs. She pounced on him unexpectedly.

"I am tired of hearing that university stuff. You promised to do everything for me after college, but I have not seen anything different. There is nothing in my box that I can point to that you bought for me since we met, not even a head tie. I would have been walking naked in the street had it not been for my mother."

"May God forbid. You will never walk naked in the street as long as I am alive. What type of husband is this that cannot buy even a rag for his wife?" Fanta's mother raged.

"Not that I do not want to buy her things, but the money I am paid cannot even sustain us up to the end of the month. I do not know the last time I bought a pair of shoes, or trousers for myself," Salieu defended.

"But you have money to buy things for other women in the street. There is no way you can explain that," Fanta's mother growled. Salieu shifted to the other end of his seat and shuffled his feet.

"I am going to ask Fanta's mother to give you a second chance," the section chief interrupted, noting the rebukes were intensifying.

"He will not change," Fanta's mother said angrily.

"You can tell a ripe corn by its look," she continued, her voice more impassioned this time.

"And, indeed, this corn is not ripe," Fanta added and laughed mockingly.

The manner in which she twisted her lips, you could literally see a twinge of embarrassment on them. She then scaled her husband several times with her eyes. Salieu turned his head away, avoiding the ruthless browbeating of his wife.

Fatima was deeply hurt by the ripping apart of his son, but she decided to keep quiet.

She knew interfering would jeopardise the chances of Fanta's mother agreeing to return the baby.

"Time will tell if he is going to change," Fanta's mother said after a brief silence.

"I will be a witness to that when he comes to me for help the next time," the section chief tried to appease the enraging mother-in-law. He then turned to Salieu and admonished him. There was a dose of seriousness in his voice.

"You have to change the way you do things if you want to keep this woman as your wife. Women are like flowers. If you do not water them, they will die."

"Since you have pleaded on his behalf, I will allow my daughter and the baby to return. Our elders say, "*God does not come down to earth and talk to us. He uses wise people like yourself to do that.* But I want him to understand that this is the last favour I am going to do for him. I have bought the crib for the baby and let him make sure that he adds it to the list of things that he owes me," Fanta's mother told the section chief.

She handed the baby to her daughter and turned to the other end of the bench, away from her son-in-law.

# CHAPTER TWENTY TWO

With the help of a college mate, Salieu got a new job as a court clerk in the provincial town of Portloko. His name was Hamjatta, an area engineer. Having a close relationship with the chief, he had made him recommend his friend to replace the previous one who died. The chief, for a reason Hamjatta could understand, was initially skeptical.

"Are you sure your friend will be willing to work with me?" The chief had asked Hamjatta several times.

"I have known him for many years, and he is not somebody you will have a problem working with."

"Your brother-in-law was a nice man and easy to work with. It is rather unfortunate he had to die this way," the chief consented.

During the time of the "voucher gate" investigation, Hamjatta's brother-in-law took the blame and lost everything just to protect the chief: he was sacked, remanded and had his properties confiscated, but for one of the houses he had kept under the name of another person. Hamjatta and his sister, the widow, now lived in that house.

When the news about his new job reached Salieu, he once again felt like a man in his household and his confidence returned. Even his mother, Fatima, was happy that her son was moving to another town. The prospect about him being able now to take care of her and his family was very gratifying. It gave her the satisfaction that she did not sacrifice everything for him in vain. Fanta's mother, however, remained reserved. She could not understand why Salieu, of all people, would relocate to another town without taking his family and sick mother along.

"He told me he would come for us after he has settled down," Fanta tried to assuage her mother.

"That is the point I will not agree with you," the mother said. "Any man that loves his family will not take a new job without thinking about his family. He should have thought about his family before taking the job," she continued.

"He said he will come for us immediately he finds a place that is big enough to accommodate all of us," Fanta continued to pacify her mother.

"And you believe that?" the mother roared and gnashed her teeth in disgust.

"Please mother, let us give him time to settle. I think it will be difficult for him to settle into his new role with all of us cramped in one tiny room," Fanta said and shrugged to indicate her final decision.

"It is your call," Fanta's mother said with an equally condescending shrug of her shoulders. She was quite amazed at the free-from-blame position her daughter had taken.

While Fanta's mother doubted the sincerity of her son-in-law's judgment, Fatima indulged herself in a slew of congratulations from friends and neighbours.

"I think my problems are over at last," she told a friend she came across in the market.

"I am happy for you. Those who have been laughing at you will now bow their heads in shame," the friend said respectfully.

"My friend, one should not die because of poverty," Fatima continued with a smile.

"Our elders say, 'As long as you are a mother, there is always hope'," the friend responded. "When are you leaving?" she asked.

"He is going ahead to find a place and he will come for us later," Fatima answered.

"I hope it won't be long," the friend said, "People will start to talk again."

"I hope so too," Fatima said, and they parted.

Before the "voucher gate" scandal exposed the dubious activities of government and local institutions, appointment as court clerk was an enviable one. The predecessor of Salieu, being famous in Portloko, led an affluent lifestyle. Many could hardly tell how an ordinary court clerk amassed such wealth. Many couldn't understand why nobody blew the whistle. Instead, being the norm, people admired. This was why many people expected a lot from Salieu. Stringent measures were now put in place to check the illegal activities, but Salieu's wife and mother took not much notice of the sneers of people who believed, no matter the circumstance workers in Sierra Leone found themselves, they would always find a way to engage in corrupt practices.

With such sensors, Salieu went to his new job. He resided in the house of his friend's sister while he looked for a place for himself and his family. Though a temporary arrangement, it took a much longer time for Salieu to find a house, but his friend understood and continued to accommodate and wait for him. During those first months of his relocation to Portloko, Salieu paid regular visits to Lunsar, bringing the necessary largess to upkeep his family. But letting his family join him in his new location became a bone of contention each time he came to visit.

"This is the sixth month since you moved, and you are still dragging your feet. When are we going to join you?" Fanta asked.

"I am still trying to settle down in my new job. I do not have any extra cash and the one I am earning at the moment is not enough to go and rent a place that will accommodate all of us."

"You are simply making excuses," Fanta countered feeling indignant. "The amount of money you spend in commuting is enough to rent a house."

By the way he dodged her gaze, Fanta came to conclusion that her husband was hiding something from her and she was determined this time to confront him and try to resolve the matter once and for all. "I will not stay here tomorrow. I am going with you to Portloko whether you like it or not."

This puzzled Salieu and he stood speechless trying to conjure the appropriate response to the demand of his determined wife. Indeed, Salieu had something he was hiding—he had involved himself with the sister of his friend and this had made it difficult to keep his promise to take his family with him to Portloko.

"You have to continue to be patient with me," he said at last.

"One month has become six months and I think I have been patient enough," Fanta responded angrily. "I know now why you are reluctant to take us to Portloko," she continued.

"I have no reason but the financial constraint I am facing at my new job," he said.

"That is the dumbest excuse I have ever heard," Fanta said, rolling her eyes. The couple argued for a long time and Fatima, who had been following the argument, intervened. She wanted the matter to be resolved because Fanta had since been accusing her of telling her son not to take them to Portloko. She had endured several insults from her because of the matter but on this matter she was right.

"You have to do something if you want this house to be in peace," Fatima told her son. "Even my friends are asking me why you have not taken your family with you to Portloko. I am tired of giving excuses on your behalf," she continued.

"I will try and do something," Salieu promised.

"Please make sure you keep your promise," Fatima pleaded.

But, Salieu's love entanglement in Portloko made it almost impossible for his family to join him there. His friend's sister, Salamatu, the owner of the house he was staying, had kept him trapped ever since he moved to Portloko. Now she had become an impediment to his plans.

"It does not make any sense for your family to relocate here," Salamatu told Salieu when he told her of the pressures from his family back home. "It will create too much tension between us. It is better for you to commute rather than them joining you," Salamatu said.

"I promised my wife and mother that they will join me after one month. It is now six months and I have no more excuses to give them," Salieu tried to reason with Salamatu.

"Promises can be broken when circumstances change," Salamatu responded. She was serious and Salieu read that in her quizzical eyes.

"The problem is, my mother is getting the heat from my wife."

"Then bring your mother," Salamatu suggested.

"My mother is not the problem," Salieu said, "My wife is the one pestering me because of her mother."

"Why is it that your mother-in-law always interferes when you have a problem with your wife?"

"She had helped us for most of the time," Salieu told Salamatu.

"That does not mean she has to disrespect you or interfere in your decision making. You have to be your own man," Salamatu said. Salieu wanted to make a rebuttal but he cautioned. He couldn't understand why he had fallen so madly in love with a woman he had known for just a short time. He couldn't also understand why he was afraid to tell her that his family should take precedence over everything. He reasoned that Salamatu was strikingly beautiful to ignore but abandoning his mother and family at this time was wrong. But the more he thought about taking the right decision the more he felt trapped in this quagmire. He looked into her eyes and read the reason her husband used to idolise and give her almost anything she had asked for. She, herself, had told him that when once she threatened to leave him, he built her a house in her village and furnished it.

While they were talking, there was a knock on the door and Salamatu gave Salieu a petulant look before she went and answered the door. It was her favourite sister-in-law, Tete, one of the numerous girlfriends of her brother, Hamjatta who had unwillingly moved to another house to give Salieu and Salamatu the privacy they had needed. Whenever Tete came to Salamatu early in the morning it always meant she'd had a fight with her brother.

"Is it my brother again?" She asked

"Who else?" Tete said despondently, "It is that same woman tormenting your brother."

"Please take it easy," she coaxed her.

"I do not know why your brother is so attached to an old woman twice his age," Tete complained and shot Salamatu a perfunctory look.

"What you have to understand is that the woman helped him a lot while he was in college and she was very instrumental in Hamjatta's securing a job. I think he does not just want to abandon the woman, at least for now," Salamatu came to the defence of her brother.

"But he has done enough for her and what bothers me most is that the woman is too controlling, and she is not carrying herself in a respectable way," Tete responded.

"Hamjatta has promised that he will leave the woman," Salamatu said.

"I have heard that several times and I am tired of playing this game with that old woman," Tete replied.

"C'mon the woman is not that old," Salamatu said and giggled childishly.

"By the way, how is Salieu doing?" Tete changed the topic. She pretended not to hear the scathing remarks from Salamatu.

"He is getting ready for work," Salamatu said, "We are still fighting about bringing his family to Portloko."

"I thought you have settled that matter already," Tete said. She also was trivialising a concern that meant so much to Salamatu.

"That was my understanding, but of late he has started fussing about the issue, especially that of his mother."

"Mama's boy," Tete said briskly.

"You got that right," Salamatu responded with a quizzical smile.

Tete wanted to further ask whether Salieu had made progress in his new job, or not; whether he had hit the jackpot or not. That was, in fact, the reason she had asked the initial question, but Salamatu had given her the answer she already was privy to. Salamatu took Tate's lead so she gave the direct answer,

"Nothing has happened yet at his job."

"Maybe he wants to be cautious. He does not want to take any unnecessary chances after the voucher gate scandal," Tate said and toyed with her fingers.

"I think the man is just too laid back. He seems to be content with what he is receiving at the moment," Salamatu said disappointingly.

"My late husband was very smart. He bought his first car three months into his job but this gentleman is almost now in his seventh month and he has done nothing. My brother was telling me about his aloof kind of approach to things, but I never took him seriously. And what bothers me most is that he wants to bring his family here."

"Things are different these days. Your brother is complaining of hard times whenever I ask him to give me money. He was very generous before and he did things for me without even asking him but now I have to pester him, constantly, before he can give me anything."

"My brother's situation is different," said Salamatu. "Salieu has the opportunity to do things if he really wants to," she ended almost in a whisper.

Tete was about to say something when Salieu appeared. He had on a broad smile, waved a goodbye and exited.

"He seems to get his wits around him," Tete finally said when Salieu was out of earshot.

"You cannot judge a book by its cover," Salamatu countered and smiled disdainfully.

The two women laughed and thought about the similar circumstances they both were in.

***

It was almost two months since the last time Salieu visited his family. During the long unexpected no-show, Fatima became the depository of Fanta's anger toward her husband. Sometimes, she would flare into uncontrollable rage for no apparent reason.

Fatima, at first, regarded the squabbles and the occasional emotional outburst as a conduit to vent out her frustration, but it continued, unabated.

"Why are you asking me," she shouted.

"But you are his wife," Fatima replied.

"Are you not her mother?" Fanta asked sharply.

"I just want to know if he is coming this weekend." Fatima said. "We have gone two days without food."

"I am not going to put any pot on the fire. If he does not come for the whole year then the fireplace will be cold for the whole year," Fanta replied.

That was how they had lived ever since Salieu stopped visiting often. The mood in the home had depended on the swings of Fanta's attitude. Fatima would wake up in the morning and gauge Fanta's attitude. Good or bad, that would be the mood she would equally be in.

# CHAPTER TWENTY THREE

Almost everybody in Moyamba knew the reckless extravagance of the bursar at Sewa Secondary School. Before the rebels invaded the town, he was very vocal in his protestation against their ruthless actions of victimising innocent people. He was confident that the rebels would not attack Moyamba and he assured the people that if they did, the government soldiers would force them out of the town. His confrontational utterances reached the higher commands of the rebels and he was placed on the list of people to be targeted. In fact, his name was marked with an asterisk as one of the people to be brought dead, or alive to the commander.

In addition to the bitterness the rebels felt towards the bursar, many of the town's people prayed daily for his demise. The day the rebels attacked Moyamba, the young rebel, who directed the others to his house, was among such group of people who had prayed for his downfall. When the bursar came out of his room, he offered the rebels money. But they wanted more and they knew he had more and so they forced it out of him, assaulting his wife and daughter.

"This is all the money that I have," the bursar pleaded.

"Then let the fun begin," Kalilu, the second son of Ya Feth, ordered his men. He had left home to join the rebels, to earn much needed money his mother could no longer give to him.

The rebels grabbed the bursar's wife and daughter and stripped them naked. His two boys frantically covered their faces, trying to avoid seeing the nakedness of their mother and sister, who now lay on the floor weeping and asking for mercy.

"Please wait, please wait," the bursar pleaded, "I think I have some more money hidden somewhere in the house."

"Where?" Kalilu thundered.

"In the bathroom."

This did not surprise Kalilu as most people kept money in the bathroom, knowing that the rebels would always avoid entering that private space. Indeed, people believed that the rebels avoided bathrooms because of a strange conviction that they contained magical powers that would render rebel intruders impotent without exception. Many people believed this myth and always kept their money and other valuable items in the bathroom. This evening, that myth proved to be inaccurate.

Without asking any further questions, the rebels stormed the bathroom. At the far corner of the ceiling, they saw a bundle and one of the rebels pulled it down. On examination, they found a huge amount of cash. Kalilu's eyes glittered in amazement because he had never seen so much money in his life. As a clairvoyant, he knew the bursar would give more money if he continued to torture him.

"I know you have more money to declare," Kalilu pressed, trying to unnerve the bursar whose roving eyes showed he was not being truthful.

"I don't think I have any more money," he said. His eyes met his wife's, lying helplessly on the floor with her daughter on her side.

"I have some money tied in the loose end of my Lappa," the bursar's wife said. She was visibly trembling, and her buttocks quivered as she spoke.

The rebels grabbed the Lappa from among the tattered clothes spread on the floor.

At the loose end of the Lappa was a tight knot hiding Le10,000.00 (Ten thousand Leones).

"You are a liar and a cheat," Kalilu growled at the bursar.

The bursar's trepidation about what the rebels would do to them; especially his thirteen-year-old daughter churned his stomach. He had heard horrible stories about young girls being ravaged by the rebels. In desperation, he tried to play into the sensibilities of Kalilu, which he knew by now, were misplaced.

"Do you have a younger sister?" He asked Kalilu.

"Why do you ask?" Kalilu growled.

"I would like you to take my daughter as your adopted sister."

Kalilu laughed heartily, his tainted molars displaying patches of intoxicating leaves.

"Nice try," he said finally, wiping the tears that had formed in his eyes.

"We do not adopt anybody; it is against our code of operation," Kalilu continued with a guileless smile. Without any warning, he then produced his revolver, shot the two boys in the head, wiped the blood that splattered on his face with the back of his hand and licked it.

"This is for lying to us," he told the bursar, who stood frozen, mouth agape, his lower lip quavering with an audible reverberation. His whole body shook with an indescribable anger, but he steeled himself. He thought of pouncing at Kalilu, but an inner voice restrained him: *"He will kill your entire family if you move."*

His wife and daughter lay on the floor bristled by the raw brutality with which the two boys were murdered. Both their chests were rising and falling, knotted with indignation that never transformed to any yelling. Their obvious state of torture clearly unnerved Kalilu and prevented him from doing the thinkable, he could not go on to Kill the entire family.

"Why are you staring at me like that," Kalilu yelled at the bursar, "you are lucky I spared your wife and daughter," he continued, his voice becoming strident.

"And I spared you...this time. It will not be so when we arrive," he stammered and ordered the bursar and the remaining of his family to follow him.

\*\*\*

Kalilu and his men returned to a quiet base, except for a few turnstiles manned by heavily built rebels with machine guns and rocket propel grenades, mounted on sandbags used as a blockade to the main entrance. Their faces were stony, and the billowing smoke of the marijuana was still visible in the air. They started making cat calls when they saw the naked women trailing the band of rebels.

After they crossed the gate, two men approached them, held the women and pulled them away. The women screamed and yelled but the men hauled them on and dragged them away. The bursar waited torturously before the brigadier emerged from his highly guarded bunker.

"Is this the famous bursar that has been badmouthing us?" the brigadier asked.

He shot a fierce look at the bursar who appeared composed because his mind was preoccupied with the fate of his wife and daughter who were dragged away a moment ago.

"Please do not harm my family," the bursar dropped to his knees pleading as effectively as possible.

"It all depends on if you are willing to work with us," the brigadier said, "We need people like you."

"I will do anything you want me to do as long as you do not harm my wife and daughter," he had a brainwave, "As a matter of fact; you look like my friend, Colonel Idrissa, of the national army." He looked up wishfully at the brigadier.

"Do you know colonel Idrissa?"

"He came to my house last week. You know he is in charge of protecting this area. In fact, he told me how tired they are now of fighting the war because the army is not getting the needed support from the government."

The brigadier shook his head repeatedly. This was invaluable information as not too long, he and his boss, Sankollo, were hinted of a serious dissension within the army, and how some senior officers were planning to publicly defy the orders of the president because of the light-handed manner in which the war was being fought. *This man knows what he is talking about*, the brigadier thought and then responded.

"The son of a bitch has been harassing my boys. How close are you to Colonel Idrissa?"

"We are very close," the bursar said, "We were friends since high school and he comes to my house every time he comes to Moyamba," he ended confidently, trying to take advantage of the evolving situation.

"Is there any way you can convince the colonel to join the rebel movement?" The brigadier asked. He was now visibly pleased with the bursar. He wore a mild smile that exposed his glistening gold plated teeth.

"He told me the last time he came to my house that they are planning a major assault on the rebels. I think I will be able to get more information from him if you allow me to go and see him."

"In that case, I will allow you to go," the brigadier quickly responded.

"But I do not have any money," the bursar said.

"I will give you some money," the brigadier said.

"What about my wife and daughter?" The bursar calmly asked.

"They will remain here, and I want to assure you that nothing will happen to them as long as you continue to cooperate with us."

"Can I please see them before I leave?" He asked nervously, scared that he was asking too much from the brigadier.

"Of course, of course," the brigadier repeated happily.

Minutes later, the bursar's wife and daughter emerged from a small house, well dressed, their hair nicely corn rowed and parted into two long braids.

*"Are they getting them ready for the boss?" "Why did they decide to get them so well-groomed the moment they took them?"* Such were the questions pricking his mind.

"I can do anything you asked of me provided you do not hurt them," the bursar finally told the brigadier.

"That will only happen if you keep your own side of the agreement," the brigadier said and smiled scornfully.

With the wave of his hand, the bursar's wife and daughter were led back into the house. The bursar's stomach churned, knowing fully well the unpredictable nature of the rebels. After receiving a pass from the brigadier, he left the base, determined to do all that was humanly possible to save his remaining family.

Arriving, he went first to Mr Coker's house and tried to recruit him, because he knew that he enjoyed the respect of many people in the town. He knew having him on his side; the people in town would listen to him and comply with the rebels.

However, Mr Coker had locked himself in his room still afraid of the threats made by Kalilu's the other day.

"Open the door or else we are going to break it," Kalilu thundered from the outside.

The teacher and his wife did not move. They lay on their stomachs resigned to their fates. Kalilu and his men smashed the wooden door open and rushed into the room. Mr Coker's wife screamed when Kalilu pointed the gun at them, with bloodshot eyes.

"Are you not the teacher?" Kalilu asked.

"Yes I am," he replied with astonishment, "Do I know you?"

"Yes, you do," Kalilu growled, "are you not the boyfriend of Fatima, my mother's mate?"

The teacher's wife ceased crying and looked at his husband disdainfully.

"She was just a friend of mine," the teacher explained.

"Shut up, you liar," Kalilu said and slapped the teacher. "If you open your mouth one more time, you will be dead." Kalilu pointed his gun at his forehead and cocked it. Martha screamed once more and pleaded.

"Then you have to give me all the satisfaction that your husband had with my step-mother, Fatima," Kalilu said and smiled mischievously.

"Please don't do this to me," she continued to plead.

"I am going to do this right in front of this cheater you call a husband," Kalilu barked.

He suddenly became hysterical, shouting, jumping and dismantling his militia gears; waistcoat and detaching grenades from each of its pockets. The other rebels came, grabbed Martha and stripped her naked. They forcefully opened her legs and Kalilu went into her. The other rebels stood by, clapping, enjoying the rhythmic movements of Kalilu's bottom and his titillating moans.

"Go commander, go commander, go commander," they thundered hilariously.

They were batty just like Kalilu, and all twelve of them had their turn, including two ten-year-old rebels. Martha lay on the floor helplessly and too ashamed to look at her shocked husband.

"How can you do this to a woman?" He kept asking the rebels.

"It's your turn," Kalilu snarled at her man who pretended not to hear.

Kalilu hit him mercilessly on the back with the butt of his gun, sending him sprawling across the floor like a child. He pointed the gun at him and growled irreverently, "I said it is your turn." The other rebels pounced on him, tore his pants and pushed him forcefully on top of his hopeless wife.

***

"We are here for the second dance," he said and asked, "Where is our wife?" But the teacher did not utter a word and his somewhat condescending look infuriated Kalilu.

"We are going to kill both of you today," he threatened. There was a knock on the door, which seemed to spook Kalilu because he was not expecting any outsider. "Who is that?" He asked.

"It's me, the bursar."

As Kalilu moved out to inquire of the intruder, the others got ready to attack. With a pointed gun, he opened the door and Kalilu saw the bursar in front of him holding a piece of paper he could recognise.

"What do you want?" Kalilu asked threateningly.

The bursar gave him the paper and after glancing at it and then at the bursar, Kalilu ordered his men to leave the premise, giving the bursar the space to carry out his plan.

"Everything will be OK," the bursar told Mr. Coker who still sat dejectedly in the only chair in his room.

"Where are the rebels?" He asked.

"They left," the bursar said with an air of importance.

"How come they listened to you so easily?" The teacher asked still amazed by the ease with which the bursar had dismissed the rebels who were about to kill him and his wife.

"They need me more than I need them. Where is Martha?"

"She is in the other room."

"They all raped me in front of my husband. I do not want to live anymore," Martha said.

She was lying on the floor still traumatised by what the rebels had done to her. The bursar's mind quickly went back to his wife and daughter he had left behind. *They will do the same to them,* he thought, and he further thought of his daughter whom he suspected was still a virgin. He visualised the bulky weight of the brigadier on top of his defenceless daughter, crying for help. He knew he had to do something to save his family and only the teacher could help him do so. But there was little hope that he would comply, and he had been brutally bruised. The bursar could see tears dripping down his face as he sat in the chair, head bowed.

"I think I will be able to help you and stop the rebels from coming to your house again," the bursar said, almost to himself.

"What do you mean?" The teacher asked, raising his head up and looking at the bursar with surprise.

"I met with the second-in-command of the rebels today. He gave me the paper that I showed to the rebels."

The teacher gave him a look as if telling him *I can't believe what I am hearing.* The bursar narrated how his two boys were shot right in front of him, and his wife and daughter taken captive. "The brigadier promised to save their lives if I agree to work in concert with them and you are the only person that can help me," he ended somberly.

"What do you want me to do?"

"If you go with me to the chiefs and other influential people of the town and convince them to join the rebels, the people will feel that the rebels are fighting for us and they will accept them," the bursar said.

"I will not be part of this madness," the teacher screamed.

"What about your family?" The bursar asked, "If you do not cooperate, they will kill you and your entire family," he warned.

"I am willing to accept that fate rather than work with those monsters," he shouted.

With his stoic resistance, the bursar left the Principal's house dispirited, but he still nursed the conviction that he would give in one day, if not for himself, but for the sake of his wife.

"*A man has to do what he has to do,*" the bursar told himself.

Apart from raping, beating of innocent people and taking away their properties, the rebels had left the town relatively intact. No houses were burned and there was no chopping of limbs, yet. Nonetheless, the streets were deserted with only few stray dogs roaming them aimlessly.

# CHAPTER TWENTY-FOUR

Fatima still could not understand why Salieu had refused to come and collect his family. The people in town started spreading all sorts of rumours once more and, this time, she could not deny the fact that, her son had refused to come and fetch them. Fanta had become more hostile to her and no one would support her to render her simple domestic assistance such as filling the water pot, used to cool water in her room. Some days, she slept without food because Fanta had refused to cook, and she often scolded her, particularly early in morning.

"Your son is having a good time with another woman and we are left in this filthy place you call a home."

"I do not think he has another woman," Fatima tried to protect her son.

"Then you will tell me why he left us here all this while."

"Maybe he is still facing difficulties in his job."

"The court clerk who just passed away built three houses in two years and your hopeless son could only buy himself a Honda bike. That is why people don't feel sorry for you; your son is not making use of the opportunity that has been given to him."

"Things are not as they used to be," Fatima countered.

"Keep defending him. All I know is that your son is hopeless," Fanta said.

'How can you call your husband hopeless?" "Fatima questioned.

"Because he is hopeless," Fanta said emphatically.

"Then why can't you find another man?" Fatima challenged, her entire body shaking. She felt humiliated, and as long as the matter was getting personal, she would defend her son no matter what people thought about him, including his wife.

"I will leave him when I want to," Fanta said and gave her mother-in-law a cold glance.

"I have heard that several times, but you are still here," Fatima teased and breathed heavily. Lately, she had suffered frequent attacks of asthma and her lump weighed her down.

"Please Fatima, sit down. You know you are not well," a passerby, carrying a bucket of water, told her.

"She does not even care about my sickness," Fatima said in a disenchanted tone slurred by her heavy breath. "She does not care whether I eat, or not."

"What do you want me to cook with?" Fanta asked spitefully, "Why can't you blame your son for your problems rather than blaming me, a poor housewife?"

"That's enough Fanta," the woman said,

"This woman is fit to be your grandmother and more so, she is the mother of your husband," she continued to reproach Fanta.

"She does not respect me one bit," Fatima complained.

"Don't you know that your husband will pay the price for what you are doing to her?" the woman warned.

"I do not care," Fanta said, flunking her hands.

"What type of world are we living in?" the woman asked, balancing the bucket on her head and tying down her Lappa well.

Though she tried to calm Fanta down, she continued to abuse her mother-in-law. This time, Fatima swore to confront Salieu on this when next he visited.

***

The day Alima saw Fatima after her visit to Freetown, she knew something was wrong. She sat on her veranda, eyes swollen, and mouth perched from the constant crying. She had good news to share with her. Her brother had arranged for her to relocate abroad, *but this was not the time to share such good news with somebody in such a devastating state,* Alima thought.

"Why are you crying again today?" She asked, but Fatima just shook her head without answering her question. She looked wrinkled and disheveled.

"Can you please tell me what happened?" Alima continued to ask.

"She nearly killed me today," Fatima said faintly, "I have not eaten since yesterday, but she does not care."

"I bought some bread for you," Alima said. She took the bread and some provisions and placed them by Fatima's chair.

"Please prepare some food for me," Fatima said, "I know I would not have stayed hungry the whole day if you were around. I do not know how to thank you for all you have done for me."

"You were very kind to me when I was young, and I am only trying to repay you for all that you have done for me."

Alima quickly prepared the food and Fatima ate ravenously and saved some, but Alima urged her to finish her food, promising to prepare more for her the next day.

"I am saving this one for my grandchild though her mother has poisoned her mind against me," Fatima explained." Ntuma," she called out.

"Why are you calling me, ma?" Ntuma asked, walking lazily to the veranda.

"I have some food for you," Fatima said.

The little girl snatched the food and rushed back indoors without thanking her grandmother.

"She is my only grandchild, and she is too young to understand what is going on," Fatima explained, grinning.

After talking about her pleasant trip to Freetown and how her brother was very nice to her, Alima felt comfortable to break the news about her brother's promise to help her go abroad, to Fatima who was now in the right frame of mind.

"My brother told me today he has arranged for me to go abroad," she said.

"This is good news. I always knew your brother will help you," Fatima said, smiling coyly.

"But I will always help you," Alima said. Fatima gave her a sublime look before nodding to her gesture.

But she knew this would be difficult with Alima living in a foreign land, far away from home. That thought made her sad. For quite some time now, Alima had become the replacement of a daughter she never had, now filling the void that Salieu had created in her heart. The couple of days she was in Freetown, Fatima missed her so much that she could barely eat food.

***

At the crack of dawn, Fanta went to Portloko as promised. She met both Salieu and her new love, Salamatu, still sleeping. It was on a Sunday morning. Salieu and his mistress

94

heard loud knocking on the door. Neither of them expected anyone to call. Though dizzy, they both concluded that the person at the door could not possibly be a friend. Rousing halfway from the bed, they both asked,

"Who is that?" Not getting a response, Salieu strolled out of the room and walked lazily to the door, yawning. As he held the key to turn it open, another knock came from the door, this time louder than the first ones. The intruder turned the knob and pushed the door. His mind ran to the threat by Fanta. Salamatu had been threatened with dire consequences if Fanta visited. Salieu swallowed several times and prepared himself for whoever this intruder could be. He anxiously opened the door and met the fiery eyes of his wife. He read indignation in them. Before he could take the next move, Fanta shouted,

"What took you so long to open the damned door?" She attempted to barge into the house, but Salieu blocked her.

"Get out of my way before I break this damned door," she shrieked. Her body shook with rage. Fearing an escalation of the incident, Salieu gave in, and Fanta stormed into the house.

"You should have informed me before coming," Salieu tried to act tough, following his wife into the living room, towel wrapped loosely around his loins.

"Inform who?" Fanta barked, infuriated by the towel Salieu had on, something he would only do when relaxing with her at home. Fanta went straight to a half open door and discovered Salamatu lying down all wrapped up in bed. Seeing the other woman lying with elegance oozing from her, Fanta started to perspire all over causing beads of sweat to stream down her face. *Take control of yourself,* she thought, exhaled and yelled,

"So this is the reason you have decided to abandon your family, including your ailing mother." Salamatu sat silent, watching the lady in front of her, whom she knew was her lover's wife.

"And who is this?" Salamatu finally asked, "Does Mrs. have any rights?" she continued scornfully.

"She is my..."

But before Salieu finished his statement, Fanta leaped forward and grabbed Salamatu. Salieu jumped on the two women, pulled Fanta from Salamatu and pushed her off the bed.

"Leave her alone and I dare her to touch me again. Are you not thankful your husband now has a decent job? You should thank me instead of attacking me," Salamatu said, rolling her eyes disdainfully.

"Decent job my foot," Fanta barked, "What benefit have I gained from his so-called decent job? You have taken both the cow and the milk and now you are telling me to thank you. Thank you for what?" she roared, cleared her throat and spat on the floor. "I should thank you for sleeping with my husband?" she continued.

"He is my husband too," Salamatu gasped.

"Since when did you become his wife?"

Salamatu grinned at Salieu, expecting him to answer the question. She knew an affirmative response from him would give legitimacy to her false assertion, but he just stood and watched.

"Does sleeping with him make you his wife? You should be ashamed of yourself. The people of Portloko will hear about this," Fanta threatened.

This made Salamatu to back down, knowing the damage such words would cause her. After the death of her husband, she was brutally condemned by the community; most blaming her for not being supportive enough of her husband, which they felt had contributed to his demise.

The court of public opinion was swift and ruthless, no matter how influential you were. *With another scandal, the people would surely share more gossip. They would not hesitate to use such a rumour in a song at the carnival this Ramadan. The people of Portloko would not take lightly to any unwarranted societal transgression.* With these thoughts tearing her mind, she ceased to react, or utter any more words, not even when Fanta threw her things out of the living room.

"Now let us see who has the right in this house," Fanta said.

Salieu tried to talk to his wife but she was too enraged to listen, and he was restrained by the fact that he was the court clerk. Doing anything foolish now would draw the attention of the neighbours.

"What do you want me to do?" Salieu asked.

"When last did you give me any money for food?"

Salieu detected a solution in his wife's response, so he went inside and took some money from his drawer and gave it to her. But Fanta needed more than just money.

"What is this?" Fanta asked.

"It is good for six months."

Fanta took the money and threw it in Salieu's face. "Tell that woman to leave now if you do not want to see danger in this house. I have been patient enough."

Salamatu was already dressed by the time Salieu entered the room. She looked at him coldly and walked past him.

"The next time I see you around my husband, I am going to pluck out your tongue from your dirty mouth. You husband snatcher," Fanta threw another salvo as Salamatu stepped out of the house.

Moments after Salamatu left the house, there was another knock on the door and Fanta rushed and opened the door to another woman, standing with a basket on her head. It was Tete, Salamatu's sister-in-law. She had brought the food that Salamatu asked her to cook for Salieu.

"And who is this?" Fanta asked Salieu.

"And who are you?" Tete asked before Salieu could answer Fanta's question.

Without answering her question, Fanta grabbed the basket and flung it to a corner of the house, spilling some of its contents.

"Where is Salamatu?" Tete asked shakily. She was now visibly shocked.

"I kicked her out," Fanta said and snapped her fingers in Tete's face.

Soon, Fanta picked up the basket, took out the food, dished some on a plate and started eating.

"This is good stuff," Fanta mumbled, her mouth full of cooked rice. "How much money did he give you to cook this good food?"

"It is none of your business," Tete said, now prepared for the palaver.

"It is my business because Salieu is my husband and your shameless friend is trying to snatch him from me. Over my dead body," Fanta said, twirled her hand over her head, snapping her fingers irritatingly.

*"This woman is crazy,"* Tete told herself.

"I will take the rest of the food to my daughter and show her the good life her father is living while we are struggling to have a decent meal," Fanta remarked, as she took the match stick lying idly by the foot of the table and started picking her teeth. She then took a mouthful of water, drank some, gargled some more and spat on the floor. She took the loose end of her Lappa and wiped her mouth.

"Are you not going to say thank you to Tete for bringing the food?" Salieu mocked.

"You can say thank you to her because she cooked the food for you, not for me," Fanta said, rolling her eyes.

"But you ate the food," Salieu continued to mock.

"By accident," Fanta hissed.

Tete watched the drama between the two, enraged that Salieu was unable to control the cheeky attitude of his wife, and left the house.

"How is my mother and daughter doing?" Salieu asked after he closed the door which Tete had left wide open.

"I know about my daughter," Fanta said, "I don't know anything about your mother," she added.

"Did you say your daughter?" Salieu asked.

"How can she be your child?" She asked.

"Yes, she is my daughter," Salieu said.

"She is not your daughter because I am the only one taking care of her while you are busy sleeping with that prostitute," she hissed.

"She is not a prostitute. She is a very decent woman and her attitude this morning tells you she is not the rude type," Salieu countered.

"She had no choice because I was ready to put my foot into her…"

"You never answered my question about my mother," Salieu changed the topic before Fanta could complete her statement.

"Am I your mother's keeper?" Fanta asked and hissed again.

"What is that supposed to mean?"

"You should be ashamed to ask me that question. If there is anybody to take care of your mother it should be you, after all she has done for you. If you want to know how she is doing, go and see her. What an ungrateful person you are," she rebuked. These statements from his wife infuriated him. He swallowed hard, trying to regain his bearing. He felt guilty but he dared not show it to her. "When are you going back?" he asked after a brief but frenzied silence.

"I did not come today to stay," Fanta said, raising her eyebrows, "I will leave the moment you give me the money."

Salieu went back into his room, brought out some more money and handed it to his wife. Fanta counted it briskly and muttered "You must be out of your mind."

"That should be just enough to upkeep the family for the next two months," he tried to reason with her.

"Our elders say, you wear a hat because you want to be tall. Do you know the cost for a pound of meat?" Fanta asked sarcastically. "From now on, I am going to eat the same food that you gave your mistress's friend to prepare for you."

"I did not give her any money," he bluffed.

"I do not know when you will start telling the truth," Fanta said, "You've become a liar these days. But what I want to tell you is that if I come back here and find that woman, or any other woman in this house you will not be able to handle that situation. You know what I can do. Please give me the money and let me go."

Salieu remained silent. He could not understand why his wife had become so unreasonably. He knew the money he had given to her was enough to feed the family for almost five months. He was not prepared to give her anymore because that suggest to her that he had plenty more. Instead, he kept quiet and continued to gaze at her. They stayed silent for some time and Fanta barked, "Are you going to give me the money, or not?"

"I will come next week and bring you more money."

"That is a deal," Fanta said in a matter-of-fact way, tucked the money into her handbag and rolled her eyes at her husband.

"Thank you," Salieu quipped.

"You do not deserve any thanks," Fanta retorted, "You are a shameless man," she added, rolled her eyes again, grabbed her bag and left, slamming the door behind her.

# CHAPTER TWENTY FIVE

Before the rebels attacked Moyamba, the Sewa Secondary School, was rated first in academic performance, sports and discipline. Mr Coker had introduced many policies that had helped to turn the mushroom school into an enviable institution. The teachers as well as the students regained their respect, not only within the confines of the school, but across the entire Southern region.

Mr Coker became the national secretary of the Teachers' Union and also a member of the Labor Congress, where he led the fight for better conditions for members. He also travelled overseas to attend International Conferences during which he made many friends who donated funds towards the building of more classrooms for the school.

This reputation was the reason the bursar wanted his support, but he had already rejected his proposal, and there was no way he could give in, at least not just yet. He went to the houseboy's house and asked him to show him the Principal's two sons. But, before he got there, the news had already reached the community that the bursar had established contact with the rebels. So when the houseboy saw him coming, he hid his children and those of the teacher's in the bathroom.

"Where are the master's boys?" He asked as if he was their father, "I want to take them to their father," he lied.

"I sent them to the village," the houseboy lied, "and in fact, he told me not to hand his children to anyone without his approval."

"I know they are here and if you do not bring them out you will pay a price for that," the bursar threatened.

Not too long after, six rebels showed up carrying A-K 47 guns. They had seen the bursar enter the house and they wanted to know why he was roaming the streets.

"What is going on here?" The leader of the group asked.

"I asked him to give me the two boys of the teacher," the bursar said.

"And who are you?" One of the rebels, the smallest in the group, growled.

The bursar took the paper the brigadier had given him and showed it to the leader of the group. After reading the permission, he gave the bursar a stern look and nodded for the others to leave. The rebels strolled out lazily and the bursar intensified his threat,

"If you do not show me where the two boys are hiding, I will call the rebels and ask them to kill you."

"They are in the bathroom with the rest of my children," the houseboy finally said.

He now looked very frightened as beads of sweat had begun forming on his forehead. The bursar rushed into the bathroom, yanked the boys from there and took them to the house of the teacher. The houseboy followed carefully behind; wanting to make sure the boys were taken to their father. When the boys saw their father, they ran and hugged him. He felt happy to see his sons since it had taken some days without seeing them, but this happy reunion was cut short when the bursar appeared.

"I brought your kids because I do not want anything to happen to them," the bursar said, glancing at their father deviously.

"Where is Mama?" The boys asked together.

"She is in the other room," the teacher answered, trying to ignore the bursar's cold gaze.

The boys slid off their father's hands and headed toward their mother who had already left her room for the veranda when she heard the shrill voices of her kids. Her face was puffy, and she leaked her chapped mouth frequently, talking to her children. She looked withered and old.

"What is wrong with you Mama?" The older boy asked. He saw that her mother was ill.

"I have been sick for a long time," she said.

"Did you take any medicine?" The other boy asked.

"The rebels took away all the medicine in the house," she said and leaked her mouth again, "And you know I cannot go to the pharmacy to get any medicine because they told us to stay indoors," she continued.

"I will go and get some medicine for you right now," the older son offered.

"It is dangerous to walk outside," she said, "And besides, they took all the money we had in the house."

"I will go and ask the bursar to give me some money so that the houseboy and I will go and get some medicine for you," the boy said and ran to speaK to the bursar in the living room.

"I need some money from you" he demanded.

"To do what?" The bursar asked surprised.

"Mama Martha is sick, and she needs some medicine."

"You cannot go out into the street, because the place is not safe. I will go and get the medicine myself," the bursar explained.

"Why can't you go and ask her what is bothering her?" The boy suggested.

"I know what is bothering her," the bursar said and left the house abruptly.

The moment the houseboy entered the house, he went straight to the kitchen to prepare some food. He knew his madam and master were starving. The bursar went to the biggest pharmacy in town and ordered the owner to give him drugs. "If you want to do business in town, you have to do what I have asked you to do," he said.

He resisted so the bursar went out and came back with a group of rebels brandishing their A-K 47s. The rebels went inside the pharmacy and took all the money, boxes of drugs and bandages. The rebels even threatened to rape the wives and daughters of the owner, but the bursar begged them not to do so. Before they left, the leader of the group rushed at the owner, slapped him and ordered,

"You have to report to the base every morning for refusing to obey the orders of the boss." He again rushed toward the owner, raised his hand but instead of hitting the owner growled, "You hear me?"

"Yes sir. I will report every morning to the base, sir" the pharmacy owner said. His left eye was blood-shot and swollen.

Not too long, the bursar came back with some medicines, gave them to Martha and left abruptly.

After Martha had taken some vitamin tablets, she strolled to her husband's room and asked him whether he was ready to eat.

"I still don't' feel like eating," The teacher said meekly.

"You have to eat something. You cannot blame yourself for what happened," Martha pleaded. "The important thing is that the boys are okay, and we should be thankful for that."

"How are you feeling now?" the teacher asked. The gory effect of that gang rape kept playing incessantly in his mind.

"I feel much better," Martha replied coyly.    "The bursar brought for us a lot of medication and some vitamin tablets, which you have to take to help your appetite," she continued. A brief awkward silence followed, and the teacher raised his head to face his wife but still couldn't stand making eye contact with her. Martha broke the silence. "I was not expecting him to be so helpful after the rift that occurred between you." The teacher made to say something, but stopped, raised his eyes and gazed at the ceiling. Since her husband kept dodging her gaze, Martha broke down and started sobbing, forcing the teacher to look at her.

"I am sorry for not being able to protect you," the teacher said resignedly. "I did not try enough," he continued, his eyes filled with tears.

"There was nothing you could have done. If you had attempted to do anything, the rebels would have killed both of us. It was wise of you to have taken that position," Martha tried to comfort her grieving husband. "Please try and eat some food." The teacher got up and went to the bathroom. He looked in the mirror and when he saw his disheveled face, it occurred to him that he had not taken a bath for a long time, his face was bushy. *What type of man am I?"* he asked himself.

After taking a hot bath, he took some vitamin tablets and forced himself to eat something. The food tasted better but he forced to swallow a couple of spoonsful, and after which he took a nap.

***

After the teacher had rejected his appeal to help him in his crusade, the bursar turned his attention to other influential people in the town. He arranged to meet some of them at his house, which was already jam-packed when he arrived that evening.

"We are under siege," he said, "and the only way we can survive is by towing the line. The government soldiers cannot protect us anymore."

"That is true," said one of the participants, "In fact the government soldiers are worse than the rebels. It is like sleeping with the enemy. They will come pretending to protect you, and then they will come back and attack in the middle of the night. We do not know who to trust anymore."

"The head of the rebels here in Moyamba has assured me that they will not burn or cut off any limb if we play by their rules," the bursar continued.

"What rules?" Another participant asked.

"When they capture any big town, they bring their own form of government, which is very strict, just as military rules; and those who dare challenge those rules are killed," the bursar explained.

There were shuffling of feet, the bursar knew he had succeeded in creating some useful fear in his audience.

"From now on, you need a pass to move from one section of the town to the other, or if you want to get out of town. We are able to gather here today without any harassment from the rebels because I told them that we are having a meeting."

"How much is the pass and where can we get one," asked an old man, chewing kola nut.

"You can get the pass from me and it is Le4, 000.00 (Four thousand Leone)." In the end many people agreed to support the bursar and buy his pass.

The rebels imposed their own form of government in each area that they captured and soon the inhabitants, who all this while hid themselves in their houses, felt comfortable to come outside, go to the market to buy and sell and shop owners opened their shops. Normal activities resumed in Moyamba snub not the reopening of schools.

Yet, the brigadier refused to hand over to him his wife and daughter. He was, however, allowed to see them on a regular basis, except that armed men stood by and watched. *I need to seek the help of a more senior officer*, the bursar resolved that evening, and his mind ran to Colonel Idrissa, the government representative, responsible for protecting the Southern Region. Early the next morning, the bursar left for Segbayma, another cosmopolitan town in the south, where colonel Idrissa served as commander.

"Colonel Idrissa has gone to Freetown," the wife of the colonel told the bursar.

"Do you know what time he will be back?" The bursar asked, disappointed that he had traveled that long and difficult road only to come and find the colonel absent. He had no intention of returning without having anything concrete to tell the brigadier.

"He's been gone for three days to collect the salaries for his division. They have not been paid for four months," the wife said. "Is it an emergency?" she then asked when she saw the look of urgency on the bursar's face.

"Sort of," the bursar replied.

"You can go and see Lieutenant Colonel Mussa. I think he might be able to help you," she suggested. "Just go to the junction and ask for him."

"That is a good idea, and thank you," the bursar said and headed the direction the lady had pointed to him.

Nightfall had arrived by the time the bursar arrived at the residence of Lieutenant Colonel Mussa. The place was like a warehouse and the bursar saw three truckloads of sixteen wheelers, driven by military officers, entering the huge compound. The bursar waited patiently for the goods to be offloaded before he contacted the fairly tall, bare-skinned, man they pointed to him as the lieutenant colonel. He reacted with surprised to see the face of an unfamiliar man asking for his attention.

"How long have you been here?"

"I've just arrived," the bursar lied.

"What can I do for you?" he asked almost sternly.

"I came to see Colonel Idrissa, but his wife told me he is out of town. I decided to come and see you," the bursar explained.

"For what?"

"I want to see if I might be able to do business with you."

"What type of business are you talking about?"

"I am from Moyamba and the mayor of the town. The rebels have allowed me to do business and I think there is a lot of business potentials in Moyamba," the bursar said in a matter-of-fact way.

"Are you a rebel?" Lieutenant-Colonel Mussa asked, cocking his eyebrows at him.

"I am not," the bursar replied quickly, startled by the sudden change in the attitude of the officer. "I act as the middleman for their business transactions. I think I will be able to help you sell anything you want to sell in Moyamba."

This got the lieutenant colonel baffled; not knowing whether to drive the stranger away or strike a deal with him. But his mind ran to their present state, he and his boss: many of the soldiers who were under their control had lost faith in the struggle, the government had not provided them the proper logistics that would help them defeat the rebels and end the war that had dragged on for five years now with no end in sight, and the rebels were gradually gaining the upper hand. This thought had pricked him and his boss's mind recently.

"We are tired of this damned war," Lieutenant-Colonel Mussa said.

"I think the rebels are tired too," the bursar said.

"Why do you say that?"

"They have stopped burning houses and maiming people. I think they want to talk," the bursar said.

"If they want peace, they should put a hold on all their activities. They are still attacking villages and towns as we speak." the lieutenant colonel said.

"I discussed that with the brigadier, but he told me that if they stopped, the government will not come to the negotiating table," the bursar explained.

"We have discussed the same issue with the government, but it is unwilling to share any power with the rebels, one of their main preconditions for any peace talks," said Lieutenant Colonel Mussa.

"The irony of the whole situation is that the government is not serious about fighting the war and they do not want any peace negotiations," he continued and gave the bursar a serious gaze.

There was a brief silence before the lieutenant colonel spoke again.

"We have to do this to survive. When the government soldiers started attacking towns and villages, I was against it but I had to accept because insubordination was gradually creeping into the rank and file of our division, adversely affecting morale."

"I can understand your situation and that is why I am here to do business with you," the bursar said. He had gained some modicum of confidence.

"You can count on me," Lieutenant-Colonel Mussa said.

With this arrangement, the bursar left in a buoyant mood. He knew he was a step closer to Colonel Idrissa, but his mind ran to the teacher, who refused to be part of his crusade. With this development, he might be able to convince him. The moment he arrived; the bursar went directly to see him. Having the support of both the rebels and the government army, all the bursar needed now was the backing of the teacher. When he came to the house the bursar brought provisions and many cooking items.

"You do not have to do this," the teacher said.

"I am just from Segbayma and it is my understanding that the soldiers themselves are tired of the war," the bursar replied.

"Why can't they stop fighting?"

"The government does not want them to stop," the bursar replied.

"I thought long and hard about what you asked me to do but I do not think I will be in position to publicly endorse the terrifying actions of the rebels."

The bursar looked at him in the eye, surprised by his sudden pronouncement.

"I'm willing to play another role," the teacher said before the bursar could utter another word.

"Which role?" The bursar asked with a sigh.

"I think everybody is tired of this war. I want to play the role of a peace maker between the government and the rebels, and the civil militias. The level of mistrust between these factions is high and the fighting will continue to kill innocent people if no effort is made to bring them together."

"The government does not want to negotiate with the rebels," the bursar argued.

"What about the rebels?" The teacher asked, "are they ready to talk peace?"

"I think they are, if the government is genuine and sincere," the bursar responded.

"If the rebels allowed me to go to Freetown, I will go and start the peace talks," the teacher said.

"You just have to leave your family here, so they know you will return."

"I don't have any problem with that as long as they are allowed to stay in this house without any further molestation."

"Okay, I will tell the rebels about this and get back to you," the bursar said and left.

# CHAPTER TWENTY SIX

When Fanta returned from Portloko, she went straight to her mother's house to pick up her daughter. She wanted to explain to her mother what had transpired in Portloko, but she knew that she would find out eventually from other people. She feared her mother would blame her for seemingly condoning the depraved actions of her husband.

Fanta's daughter came running when she saw her mother approaching.

"What is in the basket, ma" Ntuma asked, pulling the basket from her mother. "Is it for me?"

"It is for you," Fanta said.

"Please let me have some," Ntuma pleaded with her mother.

"Can you please wait? I just got here. Where is your grandmother?"

"She is inside," Ntuma said, fiddling with the cover of the bowl inside the basket.

"I told you to wait," Fanta said, spanking the child lightly on the hand.

"But I want some food," Ntuma cried.

Fanta took a bowl and spoon, served some of the food and gave it to her daughter.

"Make sure you do not swallow the bones," she warned. Ntuma grabbed the food and dashed outside.

"How was the trip," Fanta's mother asked, coming out of her room.

"I met a woman in Salieu's room," Fanta said and before her mother could comment, she explained about all that she did to the woman.

"I told you Salieu had a secret," Fanta's mother said after listening to every detail of her daughter's harrowing experience. "I knew all the time that he was up to no good. Did you tell his mother?" Her mother continued, gazing severely at her daughter.

"I have not been home yet," Fanta answered.

"Let her find out the hard way," Fanta's mother said. "I wish your father was alive," she sighed.

"How?" Fanta asked. She didn't understand what her mother meant by '*learning the hard way*'.

"If you try to explain to her, she will not reason out with you and that will result in another quarrel between the two of you. The woman's love for her son has blinded her reasoning. You know you always get the blame when there is an argument. Just go home and seal your lips," Fanta's mother advised.

"I am thinking of leaving Salieu," Fanta burst out suddenly.

"That is a silly thing to say. You have suffered enough with him and you just want to quit at this time? You do not have to do that!" Her mother admonished.

"What do you want me to do if he refuses to come back?" Fanta asked frustrated.

"Go back to him and make more trouble. You have to put sense into his thick head," her mother ordered.

"What is frightening is that he does not seem to be in his right frame of mind. I do not expect him to abandon his family, including his sick mother. Something is wrong somewhere," Fanta lamented.

"All I know is that your husband is like a tortoise. You have to put fire on his ass before he can move," the mother continued.

When Fanta left her mother's house she was still worried about the future of her marriage. She passed through the market and bought two pounds of meat and other cooking condiments, aiming to prepare a meal similar to the one she ate at her husband's house. When she arrived, Fatima was sitting in the veranda, anxiety written all over her face.

"How is Salieu?" Fatima asked, realising Fanta was not ready to say a word to her.

"Did you give me any money for my fare this morning when I left? If you want to know how your son is doing, you take a vehicle and go to Portloko," Fanta said, rolling her eyes.

"I did not ask you to roll your eyes at me," Fatima said.

"I do not want any problem with you today but if you want one, I will surely give it to you," Fanta responded, rolled her eyes again and briskly headed toward the kitchen. Not too long, Fanta shouted from inside the kitchen,

"Who took my firewood?

"Alima used the firewood to cook some food for me," Fatima responded.

"Tell that bitch to stop taking my stuff. If she wants to cook for you, let her bring her own stuff. I need my firewood right now," Fanta growled and rushed to the veranda, hands stretched out. Fatima took the money from her Lappa and gave it to her.

"I do not want your money. I need my firewood," Fanta said with exasperation.

"But you can use the money to go and buy the firewood," Fatima said, still anxious to know why her son had not visited for a long time. "You still have not told me how Salieu is doing," she added.

"Give the money to Alima and let her go and get the firewood. Even my salt was used," Fanta said, dodging Fatima's question.

"Is Salieu sick or something? You do not have to hide anything from me," Fatima said and shot a cursory look at Fanta. "Is he in some sort of trouble?"

Fanta hummed a derogatory song, snatched the money from Fatima and rushed out to buy the firewood. A moment later the smell of roasted meat came from the kitchen and Fatima knew Fanta's journey was not that fruitless, after all. Her reeling and anxieties subsided immediately. But soon Ya Rugor appeared. Fanta hated Ya Rugor because she always came around when cooking was going on and she would not leave until after the food had been eaten.

"How was your trip," Ya Rugor asked, reclining on the log by the wall of the house.

"It went well," Fanta said without raising her head.

"I can tell," Ya Rugor responded, "The soup smells good. It was good that you went. How is Salieu?"

"He is in Portloko," Fanta gave a cold reply.

Just like Fatima, Ya Rugor had only one son who left a long time ago for the diamond town of Kono. She had always anticipated his return, and like Fatima, she sat on her veranda all day long singing the songs of old. With rumours that her son had died in the mines, Ya Rugor survived through the goodwill of her neighbours. After Fanta finished cooking, she gave Ya Rugor a portion with a contorted face.

"The food is good," Ya Rugor told Fanta in a mouthful. "And thank you. I haven't eaten meat for a whole year," she continued and cracked the bones with her few old teeth.

"I am sorry for taking your firewood and salt yesterday," Alima, who suddenly appeared, pleaded to Fanta who was busy eating with her daughter from a big wooden bowl.

"Please make sure you come prepared whenever you want to do your cooking,"

Fanta remarked.

"It will not happen again," Alima said apologetically.

"I hope so," Fanta retorted and kicked the cat that had come close to her bowl of food. The ferocity of the kick spun the cat and Fatima knew such action was directed at her. She got up from her seat, strolled to the cat that had taken refuge behind the bundle of firewood and picked it up.

"I will kill you if you come near this bowl again," Fanta threatened.

Fatima took the cat into her room, not perplexed by the brazen wickedness of Fanta on the poor creature. Ya Rugor ate her food pensively, her mind running to her son who had not come to save her from such humiliation.

"Why has my son decided to neglect me?" She asked herself. The gory effect of her son's absence was a hard blow to her long-held hope that there would be someone to take care of her in her old age. Tears streamed down her face, but she waved off the horrifying thoughts and turned to Fatima who had come back to keep Alima company.

"Did you hear from Salieu?" Alima asked.

"I have not heard from him," Fatima responded dejectedly.

"I thought Fanta just came from Portloko?"

"I asked her repeatedly about my son, but she refused to answer any of my questions. I am worried. He is my only son, and I cannot understand why he is behaving this way," Fatima said.

"Why can't you go to Portloko?" She asked.

"You know my feet are bothering me." Fatima responded.

"I can go there and find out the reason why he has not visited you for a long time. Do not worry about the fare." Alima said.

"That would be nice of you," Fatima said, her lips trembling like a sick child. "This is the problem when you have one child. If that child forsakes you, you are in trouble," Fatima continued to complain.

"I do not think he will forsake you after all you have done for him," Alima tried to comfort Fatima. "Maybe something is wrong and that is why I want to go and find out."

"I do not think anything is wrong with him because his wife is cooking meat after she came from the trip. Portloko is only eighteen miles from here and I cannot imagine Salieu staying away for months without paying me a visit. He knows the condition he left me in when he visited the last time."

"That is the more reason I want to go to Portloko and find out," Alima said.

"I want to wait a little bit and see if he would come without you paying him a visit. Fanta is just from there and I am sure she told him about my condition even though she refused to answer any of my questions," Fatima said, still hopeful her son would come and rescue her.

"Please call me whenever you want me to go there and find out as long as it is not on a weekday," Alima said, looking a bit embarrassed that Fatima had not allowed her to go and find out what was keeping Salieu from visiting his mother.

"I will," Fatima said.

Two weeks passed and there was still no sign of Salieu. Fatima became worried and her mind told her something might be wrong that Fanta refused to tell her. After procrastinating the whole day, she finally made up her mind and summoned Alima.

"I will go to Portloko tomorrow and find out," Alima said.

"Please do," Fatima responded.

Early Sunday morning, Alima left for Portloko. It was not difficult to locate him. He was having breakfast with Salamatu when Alima knocked on the door.

"Who is it?" Salamatu asked.

"It's me, Alima."

Salieu was worried and Salamatu saw the uneasiness in him "Is it one of your many wives in Lunsar?" she said scornfully.

He went to the door and opened it. Alima stood, with a small bag slung on her left shoulder.

"Your mother sent me to you," she blurted, peeping at the angry eyes of the woman inside the parlour.

"Is anything wrong with her?" Salieu asked.

"Can I please talk to you in private?" Alima asked.

"You can say whatever you want to say right here," Salamatu barked, "By the way, who are you?" she continued, coming to join Salieu at the door.

"This is Alima," Salieu said.

"My mother sent her," he continued.

"About what?" Salamatu continued to question.

"She is one of the neighbours," Salieu said.

"Why didn't your mother come to Portloko herself?" Salamatu fired another question.

"She is sick that is why she could not come," Alima said, "And she wants to see you."

"I will get there next week," Salieu said.

"Have you forgotten about our planned trip to my mother's village?" Salamatu asked eyes wide open.

"I will see what I can do," Salieu answered.

Salieu left for his room and brought out money in an envelope for Alima.

"I think this will solve her problem until I get there," he told Alima. Without going any further, Alima took the money and left. She now saw what was keeping Salieu from visiting his family. She also now understood the reason Fanta was in a bitter mood after her visit. When she finally opened the envelope, the amount of money inside shocked her. *How could this man be so mean to her mother?* She pondered.

In the vehicle, her mind kept running to Salieu remained in her thoughts throughout the return journey as she reviewed the trouble, he had gotten himself into.

# CHAPTER TWENTY SEVEN

After informing his wife about wanting to act as a mediator, Mr Coker left for Freetown, to start the first phase of the peace process. While in Freetown, he contacted the minister of foreign affairs, a good friend of his, who promised to convey his message to the head of state.

At the next cabinet meeting, he brought up the matter for discussion, but no definitive decision was reached pending further discussion at the next cabinet meeting.

"This is encouraging news," Mr Coker had told the minister when he relayed the outcome at the last meeting. "I will tell the deputy leader of the rebels," he continued.

"I think the government is taking a second look, they are being careful to agree on negotiating with the rebels because of the reality on the ground," the minister told Mr Coker.

"Is it possible for me to meet the head of state before the next cabinet meeting?"

"I think that will be possible, but I have to confirm it before I give you a definite answer," the minister said.

"Please let me know as soon as you have the answer," the teacher said.

"I will," the minister responded and went on to talk about their days back in college.

The rebel insurgence and its brutal onslaught on the innocent people of Sierra Leone continued with no sign of abatement. In fact, the rebels were now gaining the upper hand as they continued to capture more towns and villages. Many young soldiers that were sent to the battlefield were killed, their spouses and children deprived of the benefits they deserved. Even those who were actively engaged in the war were not being paid, which dealt a serious blow to the morale of many soldiers who looked for outlets to vent their frustrations.

Later, these disgruntled soldiers disguised themselves into groups and attacked the very people they were sent to protect. Rumours made the rounds that the government soldiers had joined the rebels, and so citizens nicknamed them "sob-els."

On Wednesday, 29 April 1992, these sob-els, armed with machine guns and other war machines, some senior military members and their fighting brigades, stormed the capital city early in the morning. Gun shots and bomb blast were sporadic, and the citizens suspected a coup d'état was underway. Many government officials fled including the president who had a helicopter permanently stationed at State House. The officers reached the State House to register their frustration only to find it totally abandoned, so they took overpower in a bloodless coup. The officers themselves were surprised by this turn of events and immediately appointed the young captain who had boldly announced the overthrow over national radio, as military leader of the country. People came out of their houses as usual and danced to this great news because many were tired of the endemic corruption of the ousted government and their lack of will to aggressively pursue the war that had torn the country apart. Colonel Idrissa who had acted as one of the senior officers of the coup became the military commander in charge of the southern region.

The rebels had great hopes that the new government would incorporate them, but the war council of the new military government refused to negotiate and instead intensified their campaign against them. The rebels, therefore, mounted an offensive against the army and started attacking towns and villages. In Moyamba, they attacked the house of the teacher, but couldn't find him anywhere. After torturing his family to produce him, they killed his wife and two sons.

When the rebels attacked Lunsar, Fatima felt too weak to run and Alima was unable to come and rescue her. She ended up alone in her room when the rebels burned down the house. Two days later, after the rebels left, people started coming back to recover whatever the rebels had abandoned after ransacking Lunsar. Alima searched for Fatima among the people returning to the town. Not finding her, she went and searched their burnt-out house. She had a traumatic attack when she found the charred body of Fatima lying face down on the floor. She screamed at the horror and ran out of the ghost building without stopping. The neighbours came around and seeing the wrenching charred body of Fatima, mourned her passing, bitterly.

"Why did they leave her behind?" A neighbour asked.

"None of the people in the house could help her," Alima said, weeping inconsolably, "I'm sure, this would not have happened if her son had been here."

"Where is the son?" A passerby asked, his face was furrowed.

"He hasn't visited her for seven months now even after I told him his mother was sick," Alima said, tears streaming down her face.

The neighbours just shook their heads, for they knew about the painful life of deprivation Fatima had lived in order to raise and support her only surviving son.

Lightning Source UK Ltd.
Milton Keynes UK
UKHW031846221220
375699UK00009B/1240